DIFFERENT WORLDS

J†M†J

Published by Snowy Wings Publishing.
snowywingspublishing.com

Cover designed by Najla Qamber Designs.
Interior design by Key of Heart Designs.

ISBN: 978-1-946202-53-6

FOR MY SISTER

DIFFERENT WORLDS

an iamos novella

LYSSA CHIAVARI

Snowy Wings
PUBLISHING

DEAR READER,

The following novella takes place during the events of *Fourth World*, Book One of the Iamos Trilogy. It is recommended you read that book before beginning *Different Worlds*, as this will help you better understand Tamara and Henry's story.

This book also includes my award-winning short story, "The Choice," set several decades before the events of *Fourth World*. This is the first time "The Choice" is available in print, so I hope you will enjoy it.

Thank you for reading and for your support,

LYSSA CHIAVARI

SPRING

2073 C.E.

CHAPTER 1

♫

- t a m a r a -

EVERYTHING CHANGED WHEN ISAAK DISAPPEARED. EVERYTHING.

Of course, I didn't know it at the time. I didn't even realize he was gone at first, or that he was in trouble. If I had, maybe things could have been different.

If I'm honest, though, that's not even when everything changed. Really, it all started that Monday afternoon, when I got called out of my Algebra II class to go to the principal's office. That hadn't given me a heart attack or anything. I'd kind of been expecting it, what with the object currently residing in my basement—the one my friends and I had sort of "accidentally" brought home with us from the geological dig we were volunteering at on the weekends. But I was usually the sort of person that managed to avoid the principal's office, so getting a call like that at all was still enough to send my nerves all over the map.

Maybe it was nothing, I told myself. I mean, GSAF had said they were going to follow up with us about the skeleton we'd uncovered on Sunday (yeah, this wasn't exactly your typical geology project), so maybe that was all it was. A routine "tell us about what you saw and then you can go home" interview.

1

But somehow I doubted it.

My fears were confirmed when I made my way, palms sweating and heart pounding, onto the sky bridge to the administration building and found Isaak waiting for me. He told me that Joseph Condor knew about what we'd done. We had some serious covering up to do. Which was fine. I was ready to do it. I'd rehearsed my excuses all night the night before, when I'd been too worried to sleep. I was prepared for Joseph Condor.

I wasn't prepared for what else happened that day.

That moment—out there, on the bridge, Isaak and me—that's really when everything changed.

My face was still burning when I got to the administration office. The receptionist smiled at me as I came in the doorway. The nameplate on her desk read *Mrs. Finch.* "Hi," she said. "Tamara, right?"

"Yeah," I replied distractedly. I shouldn't have done that. Why had I done that? God, I'd probably ruined everything now. Stupid, stupid.

"Mr. Culver would like to see you," Mrs. Finch said. "He's in the boardroom down the hall. Are you okay, sweetie?"

"What?" I squeaked, then cursed internally. Now was not the time to be acting like a space case. Not with Joseph Condor probably listening in on everything I was saying. I needed to focus on the matter at hand, not on the idiotic thing I'd done out on the breezeway.

"Your face is really red. Do you have a fever?" Mrs. Finch came out from behind her desk, reaching her hand toward my forehead. I shrank back.

"Uh, I don't think so," I said, smiling as convincingly as I could manage. "It's probably just a sunburn or something. I've been outside a lot recently. The room down the hall?"

"Yes, down here, Tamara." I jerked my head in the direction of the voice. Mr. Culver, the Academy's principal, was leaning out the door of the third room on the right. I scooted down the hall after him, away from Mrs. Finch and her grabby hands.

"What's up, Mr. Culver?" I asked, feigning ignorance. "I got a notice that you wanted to see me."

"Not quite," said a voice from behind the principal. I didn't react, though the sound made a shiver run down my back.

"Mr. Condor," I said, smiling politely and reaching across the table to shake his hand, then the hands of the two men on either side of him. "Is there anything wrong?"

"No, no," he replied as I sank into the chair next to Mr. Culver. "Just routine. We're following up with all the students who were on site yesterday. I understand you were in Trench 21 at the time of the discovery." When I nodded, he went on, "Would you mind telling me what you saw?"

I drew a shaky breath. "Of course not. I didn't see a lot, mind you. I was in a different grid area." I'd never forget what happened, though, even if I did only catch the end of it. The person who found it was a college student, so I hadn't talked to them before. But when they figured out *what*, exactly, they'd dug up? Their scream was loud enough—if you'll excuse the expression—to wake the dead. It rang through my fitful dreams all last night. I told Joseph Condor as much.

"It kind of went nuts after that," I said. "I was completely freaked out, so I went to go find... my friends." I'd blurted it out

3

before I could stop myself, and I smiled awkwardly, hoping he wouldn't press that. So, of course, he totally did.

"Yes, your friends. Priscilla Hwang and Isaak Contreras." He smirked. "I just had a little chat with Isaak, in fact. You didn't run into him on your way over here?"

"No," I said warily. "I haven't seen Isaak since homeroom this morning."

"But you did see him last night," said Condor.

"What?"

The man on Condor's left gestured to the deskpad on the table in front of him. "Geolocation indicates Isaak Contreras, Priscilla Hwang and another student not on site yesterday, one Arun Sandhu, were at your house for most of the afternoon and evening. Isaak Contreras didn't leave until well after 9:00 PM."

My stomach lurched. Were these people *stalking* me? Was that even legal?

"I'm sorry, I didn't know it was a crime to have my friends over," I snapped.

Joseph Condor lifted his eyebrow. "You seem a bit jittery, Miss Torres."

"*Randall*-Torres," I corrected him. "I'm sorry, I'm just..." *Calm down, Tamara. There's no reason to get defensive.* I sniffled, trying to make my emotional outbursts seem a bit more convincing. "I'm not used to being in trouble."

"You're not in trouble, Tamara," Mr. Culver said hastily. "Mr. Condor here is just trying to get the facts about what happened. You haven't done anything wrong."

Condor looked like he didn't appreciate the interruption, not to mention the assertion of my innocence. But I sniffed again and smiled at the principal. "I understand. I'm sorry. We were all just kind of scared last night. Finding, you know, a dead body"—I said this heavily, for maximum sympathy points—"is awfully scary. And especially for Isaak, since his dad's been missing for so long..."

That got Joseph Condor's attention. "There's been no missing person's report filed." There was no question in his voice, but he glanced at the two men on either side of him for confirmation; one started frantically tapping on his deskpad, while the other yanked out his palmtop.

"There hasn't," I said, "because his mom thought he'd just ditched them." Which was probably true, though I wouldn't dare say that. "But he hasn't contacted Isaak at all since he left. What would you think? We all thought it. That's why he was at my house so late. My moms had him stay for dinner because they felt bad."

At the mention of my moms, Mr. Culver suddenly snapped into full defense attorney mode. He must have remembered whose corporate donations funded half the Academy's budget. "Now, now, Mr. Condor," he burst out, "I think poor Tamara has been through enough of this. She told you her story, and I must point out that she is one of our finest students, and her family are very upstanding members of our community. Surely you have all the information you need now. We shouldn't keep Tamara away from her studies any longer."

"Yeah, finals are coming up," I said, eager for the chance to escape. "The last thing I want is to bomb algebra."

Condor looked dubious, but he nodded his head. I grinned in relief, shaking his hand again before dashing out of the office as fast as my feet could carry me. I barely even glanced at Mrs. Finch on my way out the door.

I stopped on the sky bridge to catch my breath, my heart still pounding in my ears. I'd never done anything like that before. Lying to the principal, and GSAF on top of it? Even though I knew this was way more important than anything else, the guilt was crushing.

Out of habit, I slid my palmtop out of my jeans pocket and moved to text Isaak. *All clear*, I wrote. *U ok?* But I hesitated before hitting send. GSAF had known that Isaak had been at my house the night before. Could they read our text messages, too?

I looked up from my palmtop, glancing over at the place Isaak had been standing no more than twenty minutes before—when I did what I did. My face got hot again.

Stupid, stupid.

I pressed delete on the text and went back to Algebra II, deciding I would talk to Isaak later.

That was probably the stupidest thing of all.

CHAPTER 2

- h e n r y -

EVERYTHING WENT STRAIGHT TO HELL WHEN ISAAK DISAPPEARED.

I should have known something like this was going to happen. I, of all people, should have seen it coming. But of course I didn't. I was just what I'd always accused Isaak, and Tamara, and all our classmates at the Academy of being: complacent.

If I'd been thinking clearly, I would have realized something was up when Isaak didn't text me back that afternoon. But I didn't. I just figured that he didn't want to get busted texting in class. There was only an hour left before school got out; he'd text me then, and we could head over to this David Hassan guy's apartment and figure out W.T.F. was going on around here.

The only problem was, I was totally wrecked. I hadn't slept well on Saturday night because I was so torqued off at Isaak for being such a damn lapdog for GSAF. And, okay, maybe I felt a little bad for what I'd said, too. I didn't mean to be such a dick, really. It just happened sometimes.

So, yeah, that may have contributed a bit to my insomnia.

And then on top of it, I hadn't slept at all last night, either. I'd been determined to figure out who this David Hassan guy was. I couldn't shake the feeling that he was going to be the key to everything. That he would have the answers we needed. Even stronger than that, there was the insistent nagging in my mind that I knew him somehow. And that intense déjà vu sensation was doing a major number on my head.

I needed to lie down for a minute. Just rest my eyes for a little bit, until school got out and Isaak could meet me over here. Then we'd get to the bottom of this.

That was the plan, anyway. Then the next thing I knew, I was waking up and it was pitch black outside. I stared groggily at the darkness out my open window for a full minute, wondering how it had come on so fast, when I realized that my palmtop was buzzing on the nightstand beside me. An incoming call.

I fumbled for my palmtop, just registering as I started to answer it that it wasn't Isaak—but it was an address I recognized.

"Dr. Garcia?" I said, my voice still thick with sleep. Her face filled the screen, wan beneath the fluorescent lights of her garden shed-slash-lab.

"Oh, Henry, thank God. I've been trying to reach someone for hours. Is Isaak with you? Why is it so dark?"

I blinked in confusion. "No, Isaak's not here. I haven't talked to him since"—I fumbled for the lamp next to my bed, trying to do the math in my head—"I dunno. A while. I was home sick from school today." Not quite true, but good enough.

Isaak's mom let out a few choice Spanish cuss words. "If he's not with you, then where is he?" Her voice broke on the last word in a way that made me feel inexplicably guilty. "He was supposed to come straight home from school today. He's grounded for a week. Ay, when he gets home, he's going to be grounded for a hell of a lot longer than that. You're sure he's not with you? I even tried to track his palmtop, but it's showing that it's offline."

I swallowed. Now I was starting to feel worried, too. "No. I'm sorry. I texted him earlier, but the last time I actually heard back from him was last night when we were on Speculus."

"He was on Speculus last night? That boy really doesn't understand the concept of *grounded*, does he?" She laughed in a hysterical way, then pinched her nose between her fingers. "Henry, please, if you can track him down... I just want him to come home. You know what? Screw the grounding. Please. I just want him home." She was crying. Goddammit.

Lamely, I said, "I'll try to find him, Dr. Garcia." I don't know if she heard me before she disconnected. I stared numbly down at the palmtop as it blinked the time at me. 22:37. I'd been asleep a good eight hours.

What the hell, Isaak?

I pulled up my text app to see if he might have tried to get a hold of me while I was asleep, but there were no messages from him. I did have a couple from that guy I'd found on the agorist chatspace asking about that stupid coin, but he was just going to have to wait.

Dude, I texted Isaak, my thumb tapping rapidly, *where r u? ur mom just called me & flipped her shit.*

No response came. A moment later, a red X appeared on my screen. *Message delivery failure.*

My heart was pounding rapidly at this point. Something was really wrong. Where was he?

I swiped through my contacts, looking for the next likely candidate. Tamara. *Tam, have u seen Zak?* I texted.

I waited. This time the message went through, but no read

receipt followed. And no response, either. She must not have her palmtop, I reasoned with myself, trying to swallow down my panic.

I tried Scylla next. She did answer, but only to say that she hadn't been able to get in touch with them, either. I moved to respond, but then a second message came in. *Old blue eyes showed up at my dorm today. Think they're with him?*

I let out a long string of profanity. *Old Blue Eyes*—that was the ultra-original codename for Joseph Condor that Scylla had come up with on our way to the train station last night. Apparently Isaak wasn't the only one weirded out by his creepy pale eyes. If Joseph Condor had shown up at school today, who knew what had happened? Maybe he'd caught them with that ancient relic Scylla sneaked off-site yesterday. If that was the case, we were all screwed. The cops were probably on their way to my apartment right now.

I got up and started pacing around the room, raking my fingers through my hair, pulling at it anxiously. There had to be a way out of this, I just had to think—

My palmtop buzzed. I glanced down at the bed and nearly collapsed with relief. A text from Isaak.

Sorry, he wrote. *Things are kind of crazy. I'll explain when I see you. I'm on my way to DH's now. Meet me there?*

I stared at the message in disbelief. What had taken him so long? It doesn't take seven torquing hours to get from the Academy to the south side of town, which is how long it had been since school let out. *WTF's going on? Y didn't u text me?* I wrote. I hesitated for a moment, then added, my fingers shaking ever-so-slightly, *Is Tamara w/ u?*

A long pause, with nothing but gray ellipses indicating he was typing a response. Then, *Can't text. I'll tell you in person.*

I didn't like this. Something felt wrong. But he was right—we couldn't exactly text, especially if GSAF was onto us. My palmtop was pretty well encrypted, but Isaak never would let me encrypt his for fear of torquing off his mom. Regardless, the government was notorious for sucking up data from signal providers, tech companies, the whole nine yards. I wasn't quite willing to trust putting anything potentially incriminating in writing.

B there in 10, I wrote at last, pressing send before I could think twice.

I changed out of the rank-smelling clothes I'd been wearing for the last thirty-six hours and pulled on my shoes, creeping out into the hallway. Mom was working an overnight shift tonight, but Dad should be home by now. I breathed out a sigh of relief when I noticed he was snoring in the recliner in the living room, still in his factory uniform, his dastaar askew. If I was lucky, he'd stay asleep and would never even realize I was gone.

The air outside was brisk and had that gnarly boiled-cabbage smell that the south part of town got on nights when it was cool and humid. David Hassan's apartment was just a couple blocks away from mine. The skin on my arms prickled with goosebumps. I told myself it was just the cold air, but I knew it had more to do with nerves. Isaak better have a good explanation for himself. And this David Hassan better be worth the trouble.

I stopped outside the apartment building, looking up at it warily. Light streamed from a few of the windows, but for the most part it looked abandoned. I glanced at the empty street. Isaak was nowhere to be seen. Should I wait for him outside?

There was no one around, but I didn't know if anyone could see me through their windows. The last thing I wanted was for someone to call the cops because a "shifty-looking" person was hanging around outside their building—which had happened to me on more than one occasion.

I hesitated another minute, then decided to go inside. Maybe he was already waiting for me there. I paused in the stairwell to send Isaak a quick text. *I'm here, where r u?* I kept my palmtop in my hand as I climbed the stairs, but no response came.

The door to apartment 3-F was ajar. I froze when I saw it, open just the tiniest crack. "Isaak?" I said quietly. Even at that volume, my voice seemed to echo around the empty hall. My hands were sweaty as I reached for the knob and pushed the door open wide enough to stick my head in. "Isaak? Dr. Hassan?"

Nobody was here. The apartment was dark, but it smelled kind of smoky inside. I realized why when I slipped inside—there was a fire smoldering out in the fireplace. The embers glowed dimly, a deep, seething red.

I looked around me. There wasn't a whole lot of furniture, apart from a folding table in the kitchen and a beat-up looking sectional in the living room. There were more books than anything else. The wall across from the fireplace was lined with cheap fiberboard bookcases, the shelves stuffed with ancient paperbacks. I stared at these in confusion. Most people didn't have many paper books, and those that did mostly had really nice collector sets, not seventy-five-year-old mass market crap. My eyes lingered on a set of science fiction books. I recognized some of the authors here, the cult classics that I'd raised myself on: Asimov, Herbert, LeGuin. At least the dude had good taste.

Then I glanced up and saw a row of trashy romance novels above the science fiction books. Okay, maybe not.

"Anyone home?" I called out again. Silence. It was obvious that Isaak hadn't made it here yet. I probably should get out of here before David Hassan turned up and charged me with breaking and entering.

But I paused as I passed the fireplace and noticed a flash of color among the embers. I crouched, looking down at the smoldering fire. The dried spider weeds he'd been using in place of logs had crumbled down to almost nothing, but there was an unburned fragment of paper poking out of the pile of ash. A snatch of blue dress, and two embossed letters, DU. A book cover?

I glanced over my shoulder at the fiberboard shelves. Was David Hassan just keeping those books to use as kindling? Seemed a little extreme.

A noise at the door made me jump. *Shit.* I was busted now. How was I supposed to talk my way out of this one?

Before I could move, the door opened wide and I saw an unfamiliar man in a suit standing in the hallway. Too young to be David Hassan. But that could mean only one thing, and I didn't like it one bit.

"He's here, boss," the man said.

I bolted. GSAF, it had to be. We were caught. The doorway was blocked, so I launched myself toward the fire escape. The man in the doorway hurtled after me, but I was faster—at least, until I collided with another suit standing on the balcony outside. I didn't have time to recover. My fist swung wildly out at him, but he blocked me easily. We struggled for a minute, but then the first guy caught up and managed to pry me off his buddy. I was finished.

"What the hell do you guys want?" I snarled, spitting a stray hair out of my mouth.

"Ah, Mr. Sandhu," a voice said behind me. I turned slowly. A tall, narrow man stood in the shadows of the dim living room. "At last we meet. I wondered what was taking you so long." He stepped closer, the light from the street lamps outside reflecting off a pair of eerie, ice-blue eyes. This could only be one person.

Joseph Condor.

My stomach fell. We were busted. Completely and one-hundred percent busted. Was that why Isaak wasn't here? Had he been arrested? But then what about—

No. *Don't think it. Do not.*

"What are you doing here?" I asked, trying to drown out my thoughts with my own voice. "Where's Isaak?"

He lifted his eyebrow. "I was hoping you'd be able to tell me that." When I said nothing, he smiled. "I'm going to need you to come with us."

My muscles tensed. For a brief instant, I thought maybe I could do it—I could run for it. But there was no way. I couldn't get away from them now. They'd just find me again, and I'd be in even worse trouble. I nodded mutely.

I glanced up at the sky as the suits led me out of the apartment building. Through the gray haze above me, I could just make out the blinking lights of a circling helicopter. I focused on that rather than the itching in my fingers, the need to pull out my palmtop and send her one more text. To find some way to warn her, even though it was probably way too late.

Because through the whole altercation, there'd been only one thing in my mind. Even though it was terrible of me, even though Isaak was who-knows-where. I really was worried about him, worried sick. But I couldn't stop thinking about the fact that she hadn't answered me, either. And just like always, there was her name in my head, over and over and over, taking precedence over everything else. Burning my insides like acid, sending me straight to hell. Reminding me that I really was the worst torquing friend on the planet.

"Coming, Mr. Sandhu?" Joseph Condor called. He stood beside a shiny black sedan with tinted windows, holding the door to the backseat open for me.

I nodded, looking away from the blinking lights in the sky. "I'm coming."

CHAPTER 3

♫

- t a m a r a -

MY STOMACH LURCHED AS THE BOAT ROLLED OVER THE TOP OF A particularly large wave. I looked up from the deskpad on my lap where I was doing my homework. We were close to the wharf now. I tried to tell myself that my churning stomach was seasickness, but I'd never been seasick before—I took this same ferry to and from Herschel Island twice a day, five days a week, after all.

I folded the deskpad shut, zipping it into my messenger bag. There wasn't enough time to get any more homework done, anyhow. I sighed, running a sticky hand through my hair, and slid my palmtop out of my jeans pocket for the fiftieth time in half an hour.

Nothing. I hadn't heard from Isaak all afternoon. Finally, at eight o'clock, when my last music class got out and I couldn't stand the waiting any longer, I had texted him. Just a brief, unincriminating, *Everything ok?* But he didn't answer.

I got to my feet shakily as the ferry bobbed, the attendants on the dock hurrying to grab the mooring line and pull the boat up alongside. He wasn't speaking to me. That had to be it. I'd completely misunderstood everything I thought he'd been

16

hinting at the last three annums. I should never have listened to my moms and their terrible dating advice. Now I'd ruined my friendship with my best friend in the world, and for what?

The fingers of my right hand brushed my lips, gently, and my face grew hot at the memory. A huge mistake.

I almost didn't see Wyatt as I made my way up the stairs from the ferry docks. I was glancing down at my palmtop again—force stopping the messages app, just in case—and I nearly walked into him. He was leaning against the metal railing of the boardwalk across from Napoleon's Gelateria, a long, lanky figure with short blond hair and bright blue eyes. The Ponsfords lived down the block from me. His mom was lieutenant governor of Aeolis province, and with my parents' roles at AresTec, we'd spent a lot of time keeping each other company at otherwise boring functions.

"Hi, Wyatt," I said, shoving my palmtop back in my pocket. "What are you doing here?"

He straightened, a grin flashing across his face as he recognized me. "Oh, hey, Tamara. Just waiting for Shauna. Check that out." He gestured at the sky over the roof of Napoleon's. A low-flying aircraft was circling over the south part of town, its soft buzzing just barely audible over the sound of the ocean. Every once and a while, a bright beam of white poured down from its nose like a spotlight.

"A helicopter?"

"Yeah, that one's P.D. And I saw a few GSAF drones go over a little bit ago, too. They must be looking for someone."

I smiled, pulling my palmtop out of my pocket again. Wyatt loved that sort of thing. When we were younger, he used to ride his bike after fire engines, hoping to catch them in action giving someone CPR or putting a fire out or something. I think that's really what he wanted to do—be a firefighter, or a police officer. But his mom would never go for it. He came from a family of politicians, and that's what he was going to be.

Sometimes he reminded me of Isaak. A lot of times, actually. But whenever I tried to tell Isaak that he bit my head off, so I'd given up trying to force that friendship ages ago.

"Hey, I wanted to tell you," Wyatt said. I glanced up from my palmtop absently. "I heard about what happened yesterday."

I could *feel* the color drain out of my face. "Yesterday?"

"Yeah. At that geology dig."

My mind started racing. Did he know about the artifact? How could he? And more importantly, why would he care? I couldn't see—

"That skeleton they found."

"Oh. Yeah. Yeah, that," I said. I laughed in a way that I hoped sounded blasé, but more likely sounded completely hysterical. "Your mom told you?"

"Not in so many words. I may have been eavesdropping." He grinned sheepishly when I gaped at him. "It's not every day a GSAF retinue turns up at our house. Inquiring minds need to know. Is that why you got pulled out of algebra earlier?"

"Yeah."

"That's scary. Do they know who it was?"

"I have no clue," I said. It was one of the only truthful things I'd said all day.

He didn't say anything for a minute, but the silence was filled by the sound of another helicopter going over. I glanced up at it, wondering detachedly why there were so many out tonight. After it passed, he asked, "So, are you... okay?"

I shrugged. "Yeah, I'm fine. Honestly? That skeleton isn't even the weirdest thing that's happened to me the last two days."

He watched me curiously as I leaned against the railing, pulling my palmtop out of my pocket one last time to check if I had any messages. Nothing. "What's up?" Wyatt said. "You keep looking at your palmtop."

"Oh, I'm just waiting to hear from Isa—it's nothing. Never mind."

He gave me a crooked smile, one eyebrow raised. The lights from the distant helicopter blinked over his head, red and green.

I sighed, shoving my palmtop back into my jeans pocket. "Wyatt, did you ask Shauna out? Or did she ask you?"

"I asked her out. Why?"

I looked down at my shoes. "No reason. Do you think it's weird for a girl to make the first move?"

Wyatt laughed. "Of course not. This isn't Victorian times. What the heck, Tamara? Are you sure there's nothing wrong?"

"Yeah, I'm sure." I crossed my arms, shoving my hands into my armpits to keep from pulling my palmtop out of my pocket yet again.

Before Wyatt could respond, I heard a girl's voice call out our names. I glanced up to see Wyatt's girlfriend hurrying toward us, her dark curls bouncing off her shoulders with each step.

"Hey, Shauna," I said with a smile.

"Hi, Tamara! What are you doing here?"

"I ran into Wyatt coming off the ferry, and I thought I'd babysit him for you."

Shauna grinned. "I hope he didn't give you too much trouble. He gets a bit fussy if he hasn't had his nap."

"Geez, guys, I'm right here," Wyatt said in mock offense before leaning over to give her a quick kiss. My stomach twisted involuntarily.

"Well, now that he's under adult supervision, I guess I'd better get going," I said with a shaky laugh. "I still have homework to catch up on."

"Have a good night, Tam," Wyatt said as Shauna slipped her hand into his. I watched them go, heading into Napoleon's, and then started to make my way down the boardwalk to the parking lot. Isaak and Henry usually walked me from the Academy to the ferry, but my moms always sent a car to come get me in the evening. My house wasn't too far from here, or from the school; but my parents were way too overprotective to let me walk home by myself in the dark.

The air over my head rumbled once more, and I looked up again. Another torquing helicopter. What was going on, anyway?

I hesitated for a minute, wondering if I should try texting Isaak one more time. But I didn't want to seem desperate. So I jammed my hands into my pocket and made my way to the car.

It was after nine when I got home. The car started to pull straight into the garage, but I stopped it and—quickly looking around to make sure Mom was nowhere in view—jumped out and ran to the front door. Rising up on tiptoe and stretching as far as I could, I was just able to reach the top of the porch light. My fingers brushed against the key card, just where I'd told Isaak to leave it. So he had been here and gone. I wondered if he'd been able to find the artifact in Mama's basement, or if he'd left without it. I wondered why he hadn't texted me. I wondered if he was ever planning on speaking to me again.

I ran back around to the garage and pulled the car in. Messenger bag slung over my shoulder, I followed the trail of lights and sound through the house until I found my moms watching flix in the theater room.

"Hey, sweetie," Mom said, untangling herself from Mama and smiling up at me. "Did you have a good day?"

I tried to smile back, but I knew she'd be able to see the strain in my eyes. I sucked at lying in general, but especially to her. I shrugged offhandedly, trying to turn it into a half-truth. "Yeah, I'm just really tired. I didn't sleep well last night."

She smirked, and I remembered too late that Isaak had been here until after nine last night. My face got hot, and Mom's smirk deepened. "Well, try to go to bed early tonight," she said. "Do you have a lot of homework?"

"Not too bad."

"Best get to it, Pufferfish. The earlier you finish, the sooner you can hit the hay," Mama said. Her voice was light, but she was peering at me over the top of Mom's head, her expression urgent. She must have been in the basement. I suspected she would be excusing herself to the "bathroom" in about five minutes, with a side trip into my room to interrogate me about who had been rummaging through her workshop. And when I told her GSAF was on to us? She'd go apoplectic.

I wondered how long we'd be able to keep all of this from Mom. Well, if it was just Mama on her own, probably forever. She could spin a yarn a mile long without batting an eye. Too bad she hadn't passed *that* trait on to me.

I closed the theater room door behind me and headed for the staircase, but froze when the doorbell rang. I stood there, paralyzed, for thirty seconds. The chimes came again.

"Is that the door?" Mom called from the theater room.

"Yeah," I called back, my voice shaking.

"Who the hell would it be at this time of night?"

Now they were knocking, loud pounds like thunder. I scooted back into the theater room, my chest constricting with each knock. Mom had pulled her palmtop out and was looking at the security feed.

"It's the police." Her eyebrows were scrunched, drawing heavy lines across her forehead.

"What in the bleeding hell are the police doing here?" Mama asked. She sounded worried, and that fact alone made my pulse race even more. Nothing ever perturbed Mama—despite her cool exterior, Mom was the worrywart.

"I'll get it," Mom said, putting on her stoniest Executive Face. I trailed anxiously behind her as she went to the door and opened it.

Two uniformed policemen and a man in a suit stood on the front step. The suited man stepped forward, pulling a badge out of his jacket. "Bryn Torres?"

"That's me," said Mom.

"Sergeant Hiromoto, Tierra Nueva P.D. Sorry to bother you so late, ma'am, but we've got a warrant to search your home."

Mom's jaw fell open. My heart completely stopped.

Mama pushed past me, bustling to the front door. "Excuse me, what's all this about?" she demanded. Her brogue was thicker than usual, the only sign that she was nervous in any way.

Sergeant Hiromoto swallowed. He honestly looked a bit sheepish. "I'm sorry, ma'am, but we're looking for an object of interest to GSAF and we have reason to believe it might be somewhere in your home." He reached into his jacket again and withdrew his palmtop. I could see the words SEARCH WARRANT printed in bold text across the top of the screen as he held it out for Mom to read.

She stared at the screen like the words were written in a foreign language. "An object from the Kimbal dig site? Tamara, do you know anything about this?" She turned to look at me, aghast.

I'm never going to be able to lie my way out of this.

I *had* to lie my way out of this.

"No," I said, my voice miraculously steady. "We're not supposed to take anything off-site."

"You won't mind if we have a look around?" Sergeant Hiromoto asked.

I glanced at Mama, trying to swallow my panic. She didn't miss a beat. "Of course not. Come right in," she said.

I breathed a sigh of relief. Isaak had found it then. It was gone.

But what would they do to Isaak when they found him? I had a nasty suspicion that Sergeant Hiromoto was only being so polite because we lived on Bayfront Avenue and not in the south end of town. I doubted that Isaak or Henry would get this treatment. Especially not with Henry's record. My chest squeezed.

I sat quietly with my moms in the living room while Sergeant Hiromoto and the other officers fanned out throughout the house. It only took them an hour, but it felt like a million years. I couldn't think, could hardly even breathe. I just stared at my feet, trying to keep from hyperventilating.

"Everything okay?" Mama asked lightly when Sergeant Hiromoto came back up the stairs from the basement.

He smiled. "Yes, ma'am. Everything's clean. We're terribly sorry to have troubled you."

"No problem at all," she said. "Let us know if there's anything else we can do to help you out." She walked the three of them to the door.

Mom watched me intently as the sounds of Mama's pleasantries echoed back to us from the hall. I avoided her gaze.

"Well, that's all resolved," Mama said when she returned, brushing her hands off on the sides of her pants.

"Mm-hmm." Mom's voice sounded funny. She was still staring at me. "You did a pretty good job lying back there, Tamara. I don't think anyone would have caught it but me."

Damn. "Mom—" I began.

"I don't want to hear it tonight. You've still got homework, and I've got a headache like you wouldn't believe. I need a glass of wine and a bubble bath." Mama opened her mouth with a grin, but Mom cut her off. "You're not invited. And I expect the full story tomorrow, *capisce*?"

I hung my head. She stood up to leave, but Mama blocked her path.

"Bryn... Tamara didn't do anything wrong," she said in a soft voice. I glanced up at her in surprise.

Mom smiled gently. "I know."

She brushed past Mama and headed upstairs.

I didn't remember to check my palmtop again until I made it into my room at almost eleven o'clock. Five text messages had come in during the last two hours. My heart jumped up into my throat. Isaak, finally, finally...

But they weren't from Isaak. Four of them were from Scylla, each increasingly frantic. *Have you heard from Isaak? I can't get ahold of anyone. Where are you?????* The most recent one, from five minutes ago, said, *If I don't hear from you by midnight I'm coming to your house to make sure you're not dead!*

I'm not dead, I wrote, hastily pressing send. The last thing I needed was the cops showing up here *again*. But I didn't know what else to tell her, or if I should even put anything in writing, what with GSAF apparently stalking us all.

I closed out of her message and opened the next one. It was from Henry.

Tam, have u seen Zak?

It wasn't just me, then. I flipped back and forth from Henry's message to Scylla's, their meaning hitting me like ice water. No one had heard from Isaak. No one knew where he was. And the police had shown up at my house with a search warrant just hours after he'd been here.

God, where was he?

My eyes burned, and I tossed my palmtop away from myself, burying my face in my pillows. He'd been arrested. He had to have been. What was going to happen to him? What was the sentence for stealing a piece of space junk off federal land? Even if it was a classified piece of space junk, he was still a minor — maybe they would go easy on him? Surely my moms had to have lawyers...

I couldn't handle this. I was not equipped to deal with things like this.

Suddenly, irrationally, I wished Henry was here. The thought came out of nowhere, so abrupt that it took me aback with its ferocity. But Henry was used to this, more than any of us. I don't think anyone—Isaak, Scylla, or me—had really truly believed deep down that GSAF was covering anything up out there in the hills. We kept waiting for the moment when everything would resolve itself, and we could all laugh at ourselves for being silly enough to believe something so ridiculous.

But Henry—crazy, conspiracy-loving Henry—had always believed. Or maybe he just gave that impression with his unflappability. He met the unexpected head-on, with his fists bared, like he'd been anticipating it all along. Whenever I felt so panicked that I could barely think straight, Henry was there with some snide comment that made all my worries seem ridiculous. That would make me roll my eyes. That would help me breathe again.

And right now, more than anything, I needed to breathe.

I rolled over, reaching for my palmtop again. I stared down at it for a long moment. Then I texted him.

I haven't seen him. Henry, can u talk?

I waited, tracing my fingers over the painted piano keys on my palmtop skin, playing imaginary scales to keep my nerves from overwhelming me. Minutes passed, endless and silent.

He didn't answer.

CHAPTER 4

- h e n r y -

I HONESTLY EXPECTED THEM TO TAKE ME TO THE POLICE station. I'd been to the South Tierra Nueva station more times than I could count—I probably knew most of the officers there by name at this point. But, to my surprise, the driver pulled the car onto the bridge over Santos Creek, leading to downtown.

"Where are we going?" I asked.

Condor just looked at me over his shoulder from the front seat and smirked.

I knew soon enough.

GSAF headquarters was one of the tallest buildings in Tierra Nueva, surpassed only by AresTec Tower on Sparta Island. Just across the river from one another, the two skyscrapers seemed to be engaging in a staring contest. It felt very symbolic, considering how GSAF came to be—as a direct response to GalaX and their attempt to privately colonize the planet. Who was going to win for control over the province, and Mars itself? The multi-billion dollar corporation, or the united forces of Earth's governments?

The regular people of Mars never seemed to factor into the equation.

The car pulled into the loading roundabout and stopped before the darkened entrance to the building. Condor opened my door for me like some kind of damn chauffeur. I resisted the urge to say, "Thank you, Jeeves," and followed him into the building.

Lights flicked on automatically, triggered by our movement, as we entered the foyer. We took the elevator up several floors. The elevator doors swished open to a hallway that was dim and soundless. Deserted. I was surprised the building was even open at this time of night, but I guess bureaucracy never sleeps.

Condor escorted me into what looked suspiciously like a police interrogation room. Two men in suits were already waiting for us; they stood up when Condor entered. He gestured for me to take my place in the hot seat. One of the suits looked down at his deskpad while Condor fiddled around with a coffee pot on the far side of the room.

"Name, Arun Sandhu," the suit said, never looking up from the screen. "Goes by... Henry?"

His voice had the typical note of confusion to it. I sighed. "My grandpa's name. Everyone's always called me it. I've never gone by Arun." He did look up at me now. I could see the wheels turning in his head, just like they always did when people tried to figure out my ethnic background. Trying to calculate how many drops of this or that so they knew how they were supposed to treat me.

"So what do you guys want from me?" I asked wearily. "I take it you're not charging me with breaking and entering, since we skipped the cops?"

Condor turned, stirring a packet of creamer into his coffee with one of those plastic swizzle sticks. "That will come later.

First of all, we just need you to answer a few questions for us."

I sat up, drumming my fingers on the tabletop. "I'm not answering any questions without a lawyer. And shouldn't my parents be here for this?"

Condor chuckled. "Cute. I think someone with your *experience* would know that parents are no longer notified once you turn eighteen." He came up behind the suit, shifting his coffee cup to his left hand and swiping across the man's deskpad with his right. I watched his eyes scan the screen for a moment, and then he snickered. "Or maybe you think your birthday didn't count since it wasn't leap year this annum."

"Funny," I muttered sardonically. February birthdays as a rule sucked, since February was a leap month on Mars—it got cut every other annum to keep our calendar mostly lined up with Earth's. Because it didn't matter that this was a whole new planet, with its own orbital schedule; all that mattered was keeping up with Earth. My birthday was a casualty of the Gregorian dating system. "I still have a right to an attorney."

Condor slammed his coffee cup down on the table abruptly. "You have a *right* to nothing," he snapped. "Now you're going to answer our questions, or you're going to be very sorry you didn't. What do you know about the artifact that was taken from the Kimbal dig site?"

I leaned my face against my hand. "What artifact?"

"The discovery of a metallic object on-site was reported by Gilbert Saldaña on Sunday. The object was later discovered to be missing. We believe it was removed from the site."

"I don't know, I wasn't on site yesterday."

Condor pressed his lips together. "Our records show that you were at Tamara Randall-Torres' house last night with Isaak Contreras and Priscilla Hwang."

I almost reacted to that one. It was a very near thing. But years of practice helped me keep my face completely neutral. "They're my friends. I hung out with them. It happens sometimes when you're in high school and have a social life."

"Did they mention anything unusual happening at the dig site?"

"Yeah," I said. "Someone dug up a skeleton. That's pretty unusual. Especially for Mars."

He sipped his coffee. "Nothing else? No one mentioned finding anything else on the site?"

"I'm telling you, no. They didn't mention anything. We were just hanging out. I've got nothing for you." I could tell Condor was getting really sick of that answer. Tough luck for him.

He switched gears. "What were you doing in apartment 3-F this evening?"

The real question was, what was *he* doing there? "I was supposed to be meeting my friend."

"Do you know the person or persons who live in apartment 3-F?"

I hesitated. I didn't know how much they knew, but I didn't want to give away too much. If they knew we were looking for David Hassan, it wouldn't take a supergenius to figure out why. I fished for a lie I knew they'd believe.

"No," I said. "I was passing in the hallway and saw the door was open. No one seemed to be around, so I stopped to check it out. See if there was anything... *interesting* inside." The lie tasted foul in my mouth, but if GSAF was going to believe I was a thief,

I'd rather they think I stole random consumer electronics than state secrets.

Joseph Condor stared at me, then threw his head back laughing. It wasn't the response I'd been expecting. He grinned as he wiped the corner of his eye. "Do you hear that, gentlemen? We have a real piece of work in here with us."

I seethed and looked down at the grotty table.

"Where is Isaak Contreras?" said Condor.

My eyebrows raised, but I kept my eyes fixed downward. "I don't know. You tell me."

"We know he was your accomplice. You were supposed to be meeting him."

Yeah. *Supposed* to. But we were *supposed* to meet up hours before he turned up at David Hassan's apartment at all. Where had he been in the meantime? Had he known that GSAF was following him? Did they have him in the next room over, checking his answers to see if they matched up to mine?

"When is the last time you saw Isaak Contreras?"

I said nothing.

Condor clenched and unclenched his fist around the coffee cup. His fingernails left little crescent moons in the Styrofoam. "All right. I'm done with him. Take him to the station, let him be their problem."

I exhaled. I started to stand, then remembered. "What about my palmtop?" They'd taken it from me before I'd gotten in the car with them back at the apartment building.

Condor laughed humorlessly. "What about it?"

Right, then. I wouldn't be getting that back. Fat lot of good it was going to do them—I'd encrypted the hell out of it within the first hour of buying it. I just wished Isaak had let me do the same to his. He had a retina scan enabled, but anyone could bypass that. The law required a back door into all electronic devices, to aid in investigations of terrorists. All they needed was a law enforcement chip and they could get into anything that wasn't modified like mine.

I hoped Isaak didn't have anything incriminating on his palmtop.

As the suits led me back to the elevator, I glanced around the hallway, looking for any sign of life. But I didn't see or hear anything. If they were questioning Isaak right now, they weren't doing it here.

I remembered the panicked tone in Dr. Garcia's voice as she asked if I knew where he was. Isaak was still seventeen—if they'd questioned him, they should have let her know. Which meant that, as of a couple hours ago, no one had been in touch with her. I wondered if that meant they didn't have him, or if they were just flouting the rules the way they had with me.

I swallowed as the elevator doors swished shut. *Isaak... where the hell are you, man?*

CHAPTER 5

♫

- t a m a r a -

THE SUN WAS BRIGHT IN THE SKY THE NEXT MORNING WHEN I got to school, but the air was brisk and chilly. It seemed more like early fall than late spring. I was grateful for the cold this morning, though; it was pretty much the only thing keeping me awake. I felt like I was sleepwalking as I made my way up the stairs from the street. Once again, I'd slept poorly. I had nightmares all night about Joseph Condor and the police. About no one knowing where Isaak was, about Henry not answering my texts. Everything had felt like an adventure before—the coin, the arch, the mysterious artifact Scylla had uncovered. But now the consequences felt way too real, and I wish I'd never encouraged any of them in the first place.

I stopped at Isaak's locker first, on the one-in-a-million chance that he'd be there like usual. That maybe the last twenty-four hours had just been a nightmare. But of course it was shut tight. I entered his passcode into the digital lock and looked inside. Nothing seemed amiss, but there was no sign he'd been here at all today, either. I sighed, slamming the door, and turned toward C-hall where my own locker was located.

The hallway echoed with voices and laughter. I moved

through the crowd on autopilot, smiling blankly at my classmates as they passed, automatically waving when one of them said my name. I had no clue how I was going to make it through this day. I opened my locker door, unzipped my messenger bag, stared blankly at the contents inside. My head was killing me. I closed my eyes and rested my forehead against the cool metal of my locker rack.

Damn it.

"Hey."

I jolted, looking up so quickly that my forehead smacked against the top of the locker. Flinching, I glanced over to see Henry standing beside me. His face was sallow, with dark circles under his eyes. He looked like he hadn't slept in days.

"Henry!" I gasped, dropping my messenger bag and flinging my arms around his neck. He staggered backward, torso rigid with surprise. Then he awkwardly patted my shoulder with his left hand. "Where have you been?" I demanded once I finally released him. "Why didn't you answer my texts?"

"I don't have my palmtop." I gaped at him, and he shook his head, his features disappearing into the shadow of his hair. "It's a long torquing story. Have you seen Isaak this morning?"

"No. He's not answering my texts, either. I've been worried sick. Do you know what's going on? Is something wrong?"

"I..." He seemed unable to come up with a response. The panic from last night roared in my chest again, and I squeezed my eyes shut, counting my breaths like the beats of a metronome until they settled. Finally, Henry cleared his throat and said, "I'm starting to think there is. We were supposed to meet last night, but he didn't show up. But you-know-who did."

I choked. "Joseph Condor?" I whispered almost soundlessly. "But how did he know where to find you?"

He shrugged. "They're following us."

"This is ridiculous," I said, pulling at the ends of my ponytail with restless fingers. "We haven't done anything." When Henry raised his eyebrows at me, I glared. "Not anything worth this level of stalking! This is completely out of control."

"That's what I've been saying all along. And you guys all called me a conspiracy theorist."

My face burned. I wanted to protest, but he was right. We'd all thought he was silly for being so fanatically anti-GSAF. I could never have dreamed he'd actually be right, but now it was fairly obvious that the government was trying to cover something huge up. "I'm sorry," I said.

Henry nudged my shoulder. "Don't look so serious," he said. "It'll work out. And Isaak will turn up. I only just got out of the police station an hour ago, and I didn't bother going back to my apartment just to get my face chewed off by the 'rents. But you know how Isaak is. He probably went straight home like the good little boy he is, and is now receiving the *chancla* treatment. We'll laugh about it when he turns up tardy later with flip-flop marks and a two-month grounding sentence."

I grinned in spite of myself, if only at the ridiculous notion of Dr. Garcia ever using a *chancla* on anyone. "Yeah, you're probably right."

The electronic bell buzzed over our heads. "Great," Henry said. "Time for our daily indoctrination session of Earth-centric propaganda." Our first period, world history, was notorious for being Henry's least favorite class. And today, I was inclined to

35

agree with him.

"Think you'll be able to make it through one hour without starting an argument with Mr. Johnson?" I asked, shouldering my messenger bag.

He slammed my locker door shut. "It will be an effort, but I'll try."

I laughed and led the way to class.

"Well, look who's here. Long time, no see, Sandhu," Mr. Johnson said as Henry and I entered the classroom.

"I know you missed me," Henry replied. "Counting the hours until I was back by your side."

I sighed, squeezing past them and making for my own desk. Their teacher-student rivalry was legendary; they'd probably be jabbing at each other until the morning announcements were over. I slumped into my chair and glanced around the still half-empty classroom. Homeroom was the only period I shared with Henry, and it was my only class with Isaak, too. With our different study emphases—Isaak in languages, Henry in programming, me in the school's tiny performing arts department—we'd had fewer classes together every annum. As much as Henry groused, I was always glad to have this time together with them.

I tried not to let Isaak's empty desk worry me now.

"Morning, Tamara."

I looked up at Wyatt's voice. Looking considerably brighter and sunnier than I felt, Wyatt took his seat in front of me—Mr. Johnson had us arranged alphabetically, which put Wyatt, me, and Henry all on one half of the classroom while Isaak had been stuck on the other side. He complained, but he hadn't seemed to mind too much. He and Mr. Johnson shared barbs just as a side effect of his friendship with Henry, but history was one step away from archaeology, so I knew Isaak enjoyed it much more than he'd let on.

"Did you finish last night's algebra homework?" Wyatt asked.

"I did," I said. It wasn't like I'd had anything better to do to pass the time, being up practically all night. I omitted that part, though.

"I got stuck on number six. Any chance you could...?"

I smiled and pulled my deskpad out of my bag. Over our heads, the intercom pinged. "*Goooooood morning, Astronauts,*" said our vice-principal, Mr. Aguilar. The requisite groan came from the kids around me at our daily reminder of the Academy's incredibly embarrassing mascot name. Not that we even needed a mascot at all, considering the fact that—despite the regular protests of the more athletically gifted members of the student body—we didn't even have any sports teams. "*Finals are around the corner, and that means the tutoring center in the library will be open longer hours...*"

At the front of the classroom, Henry and Mr. Johnson were still arguing in stage whispers. I watched them for a minute before looking back down at my deskpad. "Okay, so for this one we needed to find the equation for the asymptotes of the hyperbola..."

Wyatt grimaced. "That definitely doesn't sound like English. Did she even tell us what an *asymptote* was?"

"*The Key Club will be holding its annual bake sale this afternoon...*"

"She did," I said. "Maybe you should think about those tutoring sessions at the library."

"You sound just like Shauna. Can I look at your notes?"

"Excuse me, guys," Mr. Johnson burst out. I jumped, looking up to find him glaring directly at me and Wyatt. The argument with Henry seemed to have reached a momentary impasse, if the teacher's red face was any indication. "The announcements are on, which means that your lips need to be zipped."

"Okay," I said. Wyatt turned around in his desk—just in time for us to hear the next announcement with perfect clarity.

"*On a more serious note, we've had some bad news about a fellow Astronaut. Junior Isaak Contreras has been reported missing...*"

A deafening roar erupted in my ears. I thought I was having a full-blown panic attack for a minute, until Mr. Johnson bellowed, "QUIET!" and I realized that the roar had come out of my classmates. The voices dropped marginally enough that I could just hear Mr. Aguilar's words if I strained.

"*...If anyone has any information about Isaak's possible whereabouts, please contact the Tierra Nueva Police Department. Their dedicated palmtop address and voice contact number will be listed in a bulletin that's expected to be issued to all electronic devices in the province sometime in the next few hours.*" His voice was deep and serious, and he no longer sounded like he was reading off a cue card when he said, "*Isaak is a beloved member of our community here at the Academy, so I'm sure I speak for everyone when I say we're all hoping for his safe return. His family are requesting that you respect their privacy during this difficult time...*"

Either the voices burbled up again at this point, or the roar in my ears really was a panic attack. All I knew was that I couldn't hear and that I was getting a serious case of tunnel vision. Henry was wrong, then. Isaak hadn't gone home. Isaak was missing. That word reverberated like a bass beat across my brain. Missing, missing, missing.

Where was he?

Wyatt had turned around again and was staring at me, but I couldn't make out his features. Still standing at the front of the classroom, Henry looked like he was going to completely throw up. Even Mr. Johnson seemed shaken.

When Mr. Aguilar said, "*Have a good day*," without the slightest hint of camp, it felt like a coffin being slammed shut. The classroom fell silent.

Henry turned on his heel. "I'm going to the bathroom," he announced to no one in particular.

Mr. Johnson didn't try to stop him. He stared out at the class for a long minute. Then, finally, he said, "Screw it. We're not working today. Study hall."

I gripped the edges of my desk, watching as my knuckles turned white. Still turned around in his seat, Wyatt put his hand on my shoulder as if to steady me. "Tamara? Did you know about this?"

I tried to answer, but my mouth wasn't working. Instead of words, a pathetic little whimper came out. He was right there in this classroom yesterday, and now he was gone. Not with GSAF. Not with the police. Gone.

I put my face down on my desk, hot tears forcing their way out through the corners of my eyes. Between last night and now, it felt like I'd been crying for days.

That was just the beginning.

CHAPTER 6

- h e n r y -

BY THE TIME I'D FINISHED PUKING MY GUTS OUT IN THE BATHROOM, first period was over. The sound of the bell echoed off the tile walls and floor, followed by dissonant voices in the hall. I wiped my mouth with the back of my hand. I supposed I couldn't stay in here any longer.

It was just because I was tired, I told myself as I shoved open the skybridge door. My next class was on the fourth floor of Tyson Hall, the monstrous chrome tower that the Academy called its STEM building. It was nothing to get sick over. Just because Isaak hadn't made it home last night didn't mean catastrophe. Maybe he'd run for it when he saw GSAF at David Hassan's apartment. Maybe he'd texted me and I didn't know it because GSAF had my palmtop.

"Did you hear on the announcements about that kid in Year Eleven? Isaak Contreras?"

I jerked alert at the sound of Isaak's name. Three guys ahead of me on the bridge were elbowing each other and laughing, talking way louder than they probably realized.

"The cops are acting like it's some kind of kidnapping or something. Yeah, right. He's one of the scholarship students, isn't he? He hangs around with that weird Indian guy that does the graffiti in the bathroom. He lives on the South Side. He's probably on the run from the law now."

"Yeah, that's what I was thinking. Did you see those helicopters last night? I bet he robbed a bank or something." They erupted in raucous laughter.

"You need to shut your goddamn traps."

The three of them snapped around to face me. I struggled to keep my breathing even, to keep from hurling myself at the bastard nearest to me and smashing his face in.

"Oh, look," the guy in the middle—a redhead with almost as many freckles on his face as pimples—said with a smirk. "Speak of the devil."

"You don't know a torquing thing about Isaak," I snarled. "So you need to stop talking like you do."

"Or what? You'll make us? If you value your scholarship, I'd think twice."

I valued my scholarship about as much as a bug under my shoe, and was about to demonstrate that with my fist when a flicker of movement at the far end of the bridge caught my eye. I only saw him for a split second before the door swung shut, but I swear he was there. Joseph Condor.

We're being followed.

I glanced back at the redheaded asshole. "I'm not wasting my time on you," I said, the words like ash on my tongue. Then I pushed past them, moving quickly for the door I'd seen the suited man through, trying to ignore the sounds of their snickers behind me.

The fourth-floor landing of Tyson was crammed with

students. I didn't see Condor anywhere, but he might be just out of my line of sight. Maybe just around that corner—

"Well, look who it is!"

I groaned at the voice. My second-period programming teacher, Sloan, was leaning out the lab door, watching me with eagle eyes. "The long-lost Henry Sandhu, back from his interplanetary voyage. How was your trip to Earth, Henry? Because that's where you've been, right? Since I don't remember the last time you've been in this classroom."

The look on his face told me clearly that there was no way I was heading anywhere except through that classroom door. I rolled my eyes and shuffled past him into the lab, shoving an SD card with my assignments for the rest of the semester on it into his hand. That, as always, shut him right up. Sloan gave me a hard time, but he'd never actually reported me to the administration. I was his best student and he knew it. I didn't need to be in the classroom to learn what he was teaching. I'd worry about showing up when we started working with something a little less preschool than Python.

I slumped into my seat, giving the girl next to me a curt nod. I hadn't been to class frequently enough to catch her name. She grimaced and looked down at her deskpad. Typical.

I didn't know what, exactly, the Academy thought these classes were going to do for me. I could probably teach most of them myself. Sometimes—most of the time, actually—I wondered what the hell I was doing here. But then I reminded myself that it was better than being force-fed the statist B.S. they taught in public school. And my grades were high enough that they couldn't do much to me, so there was also that. AresTec had been sending me internship offers for the off-terms the last two annums, and they were the school's major source of funding. Culver wasn't going to mess with that.

I jammed my earpod in and pulled up the day's module on my deskpad, but my mind was elsewhere. I needed to figure out what the hell was going on around here. I may not have had my palmtop anymore, but that didn't mean I was cut off. The first order of business when school let out would be for me to get a new one—I'd have to start pulling in some more freelance jobs to save up for that—but in the meantime, I could access my messages remotely. I had set up an encrypted mobile backup server a while ago for just such an occasion.

I opened up the dummy program I'd written last annum to automate my assignments. That way, if Sloan tried to monitor my activity, all he'd see from my deskpad was dutiful schoolwork. Then I set about my real task.

I had about a bajillion messages, and that's not an exaggeration. A dozen missed voice calls from Isaak's mom and my own parents. A few texts from Tamara and at least two dozen from Scylla, the most recent from just a few minutes ago. She was giving me live updates of just about every step she took today. I was sure my palmtop had been buzzing all night, and would probably continue to do so until the battery wore down completely. I hoped it drove those asshats at GSAF crazy.

I scrolled numbly through Scylla's texts. *Prof G canceled class today. Have you heard from Isaak? The weekday sessions at the dig got canceled too. No news from Zak? Kimbal is crawling with suits. What are they looking for, anyway? Hello??? Henry? HANK!*

I clenched my jaw. At least she hadn't called me Arun. If there was any mercy in this universe, Scylla would never find out about that family secret.

Ha. Right. As if there were any mercy in the universe.

I closed out of Scylla's messages, chewing on my lip thoughtfully. GSAF was all over Kimbal, too. So they weren't just tailing me. But what were they looking for, anyway?

I glanced at the rest of my texts. Apart from Scylla's, there were countless others from random addresses, friends of Isaak's from Speculus or from the Triple-C or from middle school who'd heard the news and wanted to know what was going on. I didn't even know where to start. I randomly tapped one from that agorist guy on Earth, asking yet again about the coin. That was so low on my list of priorities that it was almost laughable. *Sorry, bud, that coin's currently in the possession of some whack-job that I don't feel like interacting with at the moment, since, you know, my best friend's been kidnapped...*

I froze, staring at the screen blankly. *Emil.* We knew Emil had been in Isaak's house recently—he'd copped up to stealing the coin. And he still wanted the key, whatever the hell that was. What if we had it all wrong? What if GSAF wasn't behind Isaak's disappearance?

Oh my torquing God. How stupid was I?

I jumped to my feet, shoving the deskpad into my backpack without bothering to power it down.

"Where do you think you're going?" Sloan asked.

"Bathroom," I said. "I've been sick."

My voice sounded more urgent than I meant it to, which undoubtedly was damaging my reputation beyond repair. But it seemed to help my case. Rather than arguing, Sloan nodded me to the door.

Once I was free of the lab, I ran not toward the bathroom but to the stairwell. If Emil had Isaak, I couldn't afford to wait for school to get out. I needed to find him now.

The only problem was, I had no clue where to find him. But I had an idea of where to start. That would have to do.

By the time the sun went down, I was beginning to doubt the intelligence of this plan. It was true that this was the only place I'd ever seen Emil, but I had no way of knowing that he'd come here again—especially today. Especially if he really did know where Isaak was. I was probably wasting my time.

But I kept my feet planted firmly on the platform nonetheless.

ADOT security had gone past me three times in the last ten minutes, staring me down with narrowed eyes. I glared back at them. I'd been here for hours, but I wasn't going anywhere until they kicked me out.

I wasn't expecting much when the eight-twenty train pulled into the station, but then the pneumatic doors *swooshed* open and there he was. Amid the throng of commuters, a bedraggled mess of gray—gray hair, gray uniform; even his skin seemed a little gray today. He looked like he'd been through the wash, but I still knew him immediately. I waited for the crowd to disperse into the station, and then I barreled toward him.

"It's about time you turned up, you old bastard," I said, fighting to keep my voice even. Emil glanced up in surprise, his gaze sharpening with recognition. "We have some unfinished business to take care of."

He folded his arms and looked at me with beady, black eyes. "Funny. I don't remember having any business dealings with you. Just with your rather careless friend."

My fingers twitched with the need to form a fist. "Yeah? Well, your *business dealings* with Isaak have expanded to include me. And they're going to include the cops, too, if you don't tell me where he is in the next ten seconds."

He raised a furry eyebrow at me. "Well, since he's not with you, I'm assuming that he's at home doing his homework. After all, last time I checked, it is a school night."

Don't fight with him, Henry. No matter how much you want to punch him, don't do it.

"Do you live under a rock or something?" I jerked my finger toward the digital display screen over the platform. It usually just showed advertisements, but now it was playing the alert that had gone out that afternoon on a loop. "Isaak is missing. Everyone in Tierra Nueva is looking for him."

Emil's eyes clouded over momentarily as he stared at the screen. He cursed under his breath. "I should have known."

Bile rose up in my mouth. I swallowed it down. "Don't give me that. You did know. You've been stalking Isaak all semester. Now you're going to tell me where he is, right now, or—"

"Or what? You'll sic GSAF on me like you did last night? It won't bring your friend back, kid, and it will just make more trouble for the both of us."

I'd opened my mouth to snap back at him, but his words made my voice die in my throat. I worked my jaw for a moment, then said, "Last night?"

Emil just stared at me. And suddenly I realized. Those thick, black eyebrows over even darker eyes. Age had hardened him, but now I couldn't believe I hadn't realized all along.

"You're David Hassan."

He nodded, just once, and the world seemed to slide into focus.

Fuck.

"So wait," I said. "If you're David Hassan, that means Isaak was at your apartment. He must have gone there after he left Tamara's, like we'd planned originally."

"Tamara?"

"Randall-Torres," I said distractedly. "She said he must have gone by her house first, because the thing from the dig was—" I broke off and glared at him. "Never mind that. So you saw Isaak yesterday?"

He nodded. "He came to my apartment, followed by an entire GSAF retinue. They were tracking his palmtop."

I let out another F-bomb. "That's how they knew to go to Tamara's. And her mom's name is all over that thing." I tried to swallow down my panic and glanced back over at him. "So what happened when they got to your house? Did they arrest him?"

"No, he went out the fire escape. I put them off, saying that he had found my name on the internet and jumped to some incorrect conclusions. They brought me in for questioning, but there was no reason for them to disbelieve what I told them. I've managed to stay off their radar a bit more"—he quirked his eyebrow again—"nimbly than your little group of junior detectives has."

"Look, asshole, I offered to encrypt his palmtop for him. It's not my fault that he was dead set on '*not breaking the law*'." That last bit came out a lot more sarcastically than I meant it to. I jammed my hands in my pockets and moved a few paces away from him, trying to clear my head. "But if that's the case, then where is he?"

"I don't know," Emil said. "He left his palmtop in my apartment, so they couldn't track him that way, but they brought the full force out to search for him."

The helicopter I'd seen circling last night, and the ones Tamara mentioned down by the waterfront. They'd been for Isaak.

"So that means GSAF has him." My fist clenched involuntarily.

"Possibly."

"No, not *possibly*," I snapped. "What, do you think he vanished into thin air? GSAF has him. And I'm going to make them give him back."

Emil snorted. "What are you planning to do, kid, bust down their door and fight off every agent in the building until they hand him over? This isn't a Bollywood flick."

I whirled on him. *Don't hit him, don't hit him...*

"You know what, screw you, man," I snapped once I'd regained enough composure to keep from beating him senseless. "At least I'm trying. What are *you* planning to do?"

He leveled his gaze at me. "Absolutely nothing," he said. His face was somber. "There's not a damn thing you can do, kid. I tried to fight GSAF once and it cost me my career. Now I've lost all my research again. I'm not going to risk my freedom on top of it."

We stood in silence for a long minute, me quivering with fury, Emil deadly calm. In the distance, the air rumbled with the sound of another approaching train. Within a minute, we'd be swarmed by more noisy commuters freed from another day's work, happily going about their lives, oblivious to the fact that in their own city, the government had kidnapped a seventeen-year-old kid and were doing who-knows-what to him. I didn't think I could stomach it.

"Fine, then. Don't show your face around me again." I turned and stormed off the platform.

CHAPTER 7

♫

- t a m a r a -

SATURDAY EVENING, I WAS IN THE CANTOR'S BOX AT SAN MARCOS Cathedral, the main Catholic church in Tierra Nueva. My family had gone to the five o'clock Mass here for as long as I could remember, but I'd missed it the last two months because of the dig—I had to make up my lessons at Herschel in the evenings. But Professor Gomez had texted us yesterday afternoon to say that GSAF still had the site sealed for the indefinite future, so my schedule was able to get back to normal for the most part.

I flipped through the song list for the Mass as Mrs. Alcodia warmed up on the organ, playing an instrumental of the responsorial psalm in a minor key while people trickled in and took their seats in the pews. Near the main door, I could see my moms schmoozing it up with some of the old ladies on the pastoral advisory council. I drummed my fingers on the podium, humming absently along with the organ; but when I saw a tall couple with a little girl come through one of the side doors, I froze. I watched them for a moment, and then whispered to Mrs. Alcodia, "I'll be right back."

I hurried over to them just as they were starting to sit. The little girl saw me first, and she grinned wide, flashing a row of mostly-missing teeth. "Tamara!" she cried, hopping off the bench and throwing her arms around my knees.

"Hi, Celeste," I said, hugging her back. I glanced over at her mom—Isaak's mom. "Dr. Garcia, how are you?"

She'd tried to cover it with makeup, but close up, I could see that her face was lined with worry, dark circles pulling the corners of her eyes down like iron weights. "Hi, Tamara. About as well as can be expected." She forced a smile for me, and beside her, Dr. Gomez nodded.

Celeste slipped her hand into mine, drawing me closer to the family. There was something unreal about seeing them here without Isaak. The dark clothes all three of them were wearing, the organ music echoing around us against the backdrop of the cathedral's stained glass windows—it made me suddenly feel like I was attending a funeral rather than a regular Mass. Despair started to claw its way into my chest.

He's not dead, I reminded myself.

"Have you had any news?" I asked.

She sighed heavily. "None. I don't suppose you know anything?"

I shook my head.

"The police say they're doing everything they can. I just can't believe Isaak would run away, but..." She looked down at Celeste, like she was debating whether she should say this in front of her. Celeste looked unblinkingly back at her with wide, dark eyes. "He was so worried about his father after what happened on Sunday. At this point, I'm starting to think he went to go look for him. But why didn't he talk to me about it? Rather than up and *leaving*? Just like..."

She trailed off. I knew what she meant. *Just like Raymond.* Isaak's dad.

I swallowed. Isaak's dad had something to do with it—he had to have—but I didn't believe that Isaak had hopped on a ship back to Earth looking for him. The answers he was looking for were here on Mars. After what Henry told Scylla and me about his conversation with Emil, I was convinced of it. But that meant, without a doubt, that GSAF was involved. And how many resources were the police going to put into looking for Isaak when the government itself was involved in his disappearance? Anger growled in the pit of my stomach. Maybe GSAF was content to let Isaak stay missing, but the rest of us weren't going to give up without a fight.

At the back of the church, I saw Father Alvarez gesturing for my attention. They were ready to start the Mass, which meant I couldn't keep chatting any longer.

I glanced apologetically at Isaak's mom, and she nodded at me. I detached myself from Celeste, then paused. "He'll be back soon," I said with more confidence than I felt. "I'm sure of it."

She smiled and sat, patting the seat next to her for Celeste. I turned and hurried up the side aisle back to the cantor's box, quickly genuflecting in front of the altar and crossing myself, whispering a small prayer. When I stood, I squared my shoulders. I was more determined than ever now.

GSAF might not want to give him up willingly, but Henry, Scylla and I had a plan. And I hadn't been about to tell Isaak's mom, but it was starting tomorrow. We'd have answers for her soon. I knew we would.

Sunday morning, bright and early, I met Scylla at the maglev station on Sparta Island.

"Do you have the signs?" I asked her.

"Yup." She brandished a rolled tube of posterboard. I could just see the glitter-encrusted corner of a K poking out of the roll.

"Was the glitter really necessary?" I said. "This isn't a student council election." She and I had spent yesterday afternoon making signs, but she'd brought them back to her dorm to add some *finishing touches*—apparently of the sparkling variety.

"We want something that will catch people's eye," Scylla said. She held the tube out to me.

"If you say so."

"Trust me." She winked. "I know what I'm talking about. Today's the day we'll get answers."

I smiled and tucked the posters under my arm. She was right. After all, this whole protest thing had been her idea. Henry hadn't come to school on Wednesday, and I'd barely made it through the day, I was so worried that whatever black hole had swallowed Isaak up had taken him, too. So that afternoon, I skipped my classes at Herschel and texted Scylla to take the maglev over and meet me at his apartment.

To my relief, he'd been there, holed up in his room doing who-knows-what on Speculus. "*Looking for answers*," whatever that meant. But my relief was short-lived once he told us about his conversation with Emil.

"I realized later, if Isaak left his palmtop at Emil's house when GSAF showed up, that means he wasn't the one who texted me on Monday night. It had to have been GSAF," he'd said.

"But why?" I'd asked.

"To lure Henry over there," Scylla said, her dark eyes narrowed. "To trap him. To trap all of us."

I exhaled shakily. That meant GSAF was behind all of this. They had to have Isaak. But the thing that didn't make any sense was *why*. Why were they holding him hostage? Was it about the artifact at the dig site? I didn't understand how anything so small could be so important, but all the signs seemed to point to it. What was that thing, anyway? And what were they covering up?

It was clear we were never going to find answers on our own. If we ever wanted them to release Isaak, we needed to force GSAF's hand. That's when Scylla had suggested we hold a public demonstration. If the people of Tierra Nueva knew what was going on, GSAF would have no choice but to tell the truth.

"There's nothing to it," Scylla said eagerly. "My parents were student activists in college. They attended all sorts of protests, and they were really able to effect change that way."

Henry scoffed. "Oh, yeah, easy as pie. Because the authorities definitely have not been known to shut down peaceful protests in hazardous-to-your-health ways."

"Do you have a better suggestion?" Scylla snapped.

He glowered.

"I think it's worth a try, Henry," I said. "Scylla's right, it's our best option right now."

Henry had seemed unconvinced, but I had to believe that everything would work out. After all, there had to be a reasonable explanation for all of this. Joseph Condor may have been creepy, but not everyone who worked for GSAF was shady—look at Wyatt's mom. Once the public knew what was going on, they'd have to rein in Condor, and then everything would be fine.

I smiled and nodded to myself. Scylla was right. Today we'd get answers.

As we were crossing the walking bridge from Sparta Island, she stopped abruptly and reached into her pockets. "Oh, before I forget, here," she said. "I made you this."

"What is it?" I peered in confusion at the piece of red braided yarn she stuffed into my hand. "A friendship bracelet?"

She blushed. "Sort of. It's more like... a symbol. Of what we're fighting for. I thought it would be fresh if all of us that are here today could wear something like this."

I fumbled to tie it around my wrist. "You made enough for everyone?"

"I think so. I made about a hundred."

I raised my eyebrows. "Do you think that many people are going to turn up?"

"Well, I posted about it on the Kimbal student chatspace yesterday," Scylla said cheerfully, "so I bet a bunch of them are here today."

On the other side of the bridge, I could see that a small crowd had amassed at the entrance to the riverfront park. There definitely weren't a hundred of them, that was for sure. "Those don't look like college students to me," I said, my eyes moving over the group as we got closer. They looked my age—or younger. Most of them were wearing pop culture t-shirts in a myriad of neon colors. A few had detached themselves from the group and were playing an AR game on their palmtops. One had actually brought her Speculus headset and was wearing it right in the middle of the park. I was beginning to think we'd accidentally set our meeting location at the same spot as a gaming club when I noticed Henry standing in the midst of the cluster. I hurried over to him.

"Henry, who are all these people?" I whispered, pulling him aside and glancing at a heavy-set boy wearing a black shirt that read *Dracula Sucks*. He grinned at me, exposing a mouthful of braces. I smiled back awkwardly.

Henry bumped fists with him, then turned back to me and Scylla. "It's the guys from the Triple-C at our old middle school."

"The Triple-C?" Scylla asked.

"The Cult Classics Club," I said, suddenly remembering Isaak mentioning the club he and Henry had been in at their old school. He had tried to start a branch when we were freshmen at the Academy—I'd signed the charter form for him, because they needed at least five interested members, even though my enthusiasm for old 2-D horror flix was much more fleeting than his—but the administration declined it. He'd been mad at first, but he seemed to lose interest once everything with his dad had happened.

"You've got to be kidding me," Scylla said. "You couldn't find anyone to show up besides these rejects from an anime convention?"

"Excellent point, Ms. 'I Named Myself After A Monster From Greek Mythology, Which Is Not Geeky At All'," Henry said. "But these are Isaak's friends, too. He didn't just hang around with rich snobs who'd only associate with him if they didn't know he lived on the south side."

I tried not to let his words smart. He didn't mean me, I knew he didn't.

"Are these the only people coming today?" I asked. I'd hoped for a bigger group than this. I didn't know how much attention GSAF was going to pay to two dozen teenage nerds wearing friendship bracelets and waving glitter-covered posterboard.

"No, there's a group from one of my an-cap chatspaces that said they'd come, too. So maybe about ten more people."

"Are you torquing kidding me?" Scylla said. "That's it?"

"What about the people from Kimbal?" I asked. "Have you checked the replies to your post?"

Scylla frowned, pulling out her palmtop. "There were a few last night who sounded interested, but then Grant got on there and started badmouthing Isaak for messing with the dig site in the first place." She swiped a few times and sighed. "Now it's just devolved into a name-calling contest."

"Great. So we can forget about any of them coming. A-plus job there, Scylla." Henry folded his arms across his chest.

"Maybe not," I said, inserting myself between them before they started to fight. Scylla already looked like she was going to blow her stack. "I mean, you know how insufferable Grant is. How many people are going to listen to him, anyway? Maybe people are planning on showing up but just didn't post about it."

Henry made a noise in the back of his throat but dropped it when I glared at him. Satisfied, I pulled the rubber band off the tube and started unrolling signs to hand out.

"Oh, real cute," Henry said as I passed one of the glittery posters to him. "I'm not holding this." He tossed it to the braces kid.

While I waited for the AR gamers to look away from their palmtops long enough to take a sign, a second group of about half a dozen people crossing the bridge from Sparta Island caught my eye. These people were a lot older—and they had signs of their own already, though I noticed as they drew closer that they seemed to have less to do with *Where's Isaak?* and more to do with *Smash the State!* I frowned.

"PunjabiAnarchist?" a man with thick, curly brown hair and glasses asked, looking at our group dubiously.

Henry stepped forward. "That's me."

The man reached to shake his hand. "Nice to meet you. ProLibertate. Are you guys ready to get started?"

"I think we might be waiting for a few more people," Scylla quickly said, trying unsuccessfully to mask her horror at the new arrivals. "Let me check my messages one last time to see if anyone else posted."

"No problem," ProLibertate said. "We'll be here all day." He nodded to the woman on his left, a blonde wearing a t-shirt like one I'd seen Henry wear before: *Free Mars*. They moved to the sidewalk, stopping a group of tourists that was walking past and handing them a flyer of some kind.

I whirled on him. "Henry, what the heck?"

He shrugged. "We needed people."

"Yeah, but these people are all weird! No one is going to pay attention to us if they think we're just a group of whack-jobs!"

"Thanks so much, Tamara," Henry said, looking more hurt than I would have expected. "I'm so glad you think I'm weird."

"I never said *you* were weird!"

"Just all the people I hang out with. How exactly are they any different from me?"

"But you're—I mean..." I jabbered nonsensically for a

moment. It was true that Henry seemed to make a living out of spouting anti-authoritarian tirades every chance he got. And yeah, he did have a healthy love for horror flix and video games. But that didn't mean—

I don't know. Henry was different. But I guess that was just because I *knew* him.

"Fine. I'm sorry. But..." I watched the new arrivals proselytizing on the sidewalk like a bunch of airport missionaries. "They do understand today is about Isaak, right?"

"Of course," Henry said. He glanced over at them himself. "I think."

Scylla trudged up to us, her palmtop still in hand. "I don't think anyone else is coming. So I guess this is it." She looked forlornly over at the AR gamers, still off in their own little world. "Maybe we should say something to them before we get started."

"Be my guest. This was your idea, remember?"

Scylla shifted uncomfortably. "Yeah, but these people are all your friends."

He looked from her to me and sighed. "Fine." He cupped his hands around his mouth. "Okay, everyone, can you give me your attention for a sec?"

The group congregated around us. The girl with the Speculus headset finally emerged, and I saw that her bangs were streaked bubblegum pink.

"Hey, everybody. I'm Henry... a.k.a. PunjabiAnarchist." He ran a hand through his hair awkwardly, like he always did when he was nervous. "Anyway, I know some of you guys are here because you're friends with Isaak, and some of you are here because you're *not* friends with GSAF. The point is, we're all here for the same thing. My buddy Isaak Contreras disappeared on Monday night, and the last people who saw him were government agents. It doesn't take a supergenius to figure out what's probably going on. But GSAF isn't copping to anything, so our goal today is to try to raise public awareness and get Isaak home."

The pink-haired girl spoke up. "But, Henry, what does GSAF want with Isaak, anyway? What did he do?"

I glanced at Henry in alarm, but he didn't miss a beat. He'd been waiting for that question. "Isaak was on a school project with us out in the foothills, and we found a piece of space junk that GSAF didn't want the rest of the colony to know about. We don't have any more details than that, but all we can think is that he accidentally found out too much, so GSAF needed to silence him."

The group erupted in murmurs. "*What do you think it was, a weapon?*" "*It would have to be, why else would they care so much?*" "*Shady as hell.*"

"Right, so... I guess let's get started," Scylla said. She picked up her sign and hurried over to the sidewalk.

Following Scylla, we started marching along the perimeter of the park. Once we got going, I noticed everyone's nerves seemed to have vanished. Scylla got us started with a chant. It was pretty basic—"*What do we want?*" "*Isaak!*" "*When do we want him?*" "*Now!*"—but it seemed to get the message across. Groups of tourists and picnickers stopped to watch us. A few approached the group to ask what we were marching for.

But when we got to the corner of Water Street and started to circle back around, a police officer approached the group. I recognized him as one of the men who'd been with Sergeant

Hiromoto, and my stomach twisted. I shrank behind Henry, hoping he wouldn't recognize me.

"Hey, everyone," the man said. "I'm going to have to ask you guys to move away from the park."

Scylla looked flabbergasted. "But why?"

"You're causing a disturbance for the tourists who are trying to get a view of Sparta Island."

"Oh, no, not that," Henry said. "How inconvenient for them. Surely much more inconvenient than fact that our *friend* is *missing*."

The cop frowned, putting his hand on a leather pouch on his belt. I didn't know what he was reaching for, but I didn't want to find out. "Henry, come on," I said, inserting myself between him and the police officer. "Just do what he says. He's not making us go home, he just wants us to move. We can cooperate a little."

Henry looked like he was about to burst a blood vessel in his forehead. But he stared at me for a long moment, his eyes hooded by the thick curtain of his hair, and his expression seemed to soften. "All right," he said finally. "Come on, guys. We're moving."

The cop led us a few blocks away, to a quiet area on Third Street. The street was silent—most of this part of downtown were offices that seemed to be closed for the weekend, apart from a bank branch that was open on Sundays until two. One of the tellers stared out the door at us when we passed. I smiled at her, but she glared and pulled the door shut.

"Are you torquing kidding me?" Henry snapped at the police officer, looking the street up and down. "There's no one here! What's the point of a protest if there's no one around to hear it?"

"This is a designated free speech zone. If people want to hear what you have to say, they'll come to you," the officer said.

ProLibertate squared his shoulders. "Free speech can't be limited to the areas you designate. It's a fundamental human right—"

"Listen, buddy, I'm getting really tired of arguing with you guys," the officer interrupted. "The law is the law, and it's my job to make sure you follow it. I'm not here to quibble politics with you. If you have a problem, write a letter to the governor."

The blonde wearing the *Free Mars* t-shirt laughed, folding her arms across her chest. "That's cute. He's not accountable to us, we can't even vote."

This was getting us nowhere. I gritted my teeth. "Come on, guys. Today isn't about your little libertarian moment, it's about Isaak. Can we please get back to the matter at hand?"

Free Mars narrowed her eyes at me, but she didn't argue.

Scylla started in with the chanting again, and we started our march back and forth down the one block of Third Street that the policeman had indicated was the proper space for us. I tried to not let the fact that there was *literally no one here* get me down. People would come. This was just an off time.

Sure enough, after a few minutes, two women maybe ten years older than my moms came around the corner. They stopped in front of the bank, watching the group and whispering. I casually detached myself from the crowd and moved sideways in their direction.

"Excuse me, dear, but what are you kids doing here?" one asked me.

I smiled, pulling out my palmtop and bringing up a picture of

Isaak. "We're raising awareness about our friend Isaak. He disappeared earlier this week—"

The shorter woman took my palmtop out of my hand, peering at the picture. "Ah, yes," the taller woman said. "I heard about that on the news." She glanced warily at ProLibertate as he marched past, carrying a sign that read, *End GSAF's Reign of Terror!* "But I don't see what GSAF has to do with any of this."

"Well," I said, "you see—"

The shorter woman thrust my palmtop back at me. "Yes, why would GSAF be interested in a teenage boy? Was he selling drugs?"

"What? No, of course not!"

The woman glared, this time at Henry. "I wouldn't be too sure of that, dear." Before I could say anything else, she and her friend walked into the bank. I stared after them, stunned.

"Ignore them," Scylla said, hooking her arm through mine. I hadn't noticed her approach. "There's always going to be stupid people. Come on." She pulled me back into the line.

After an hour, we'd finally managed to get some attention. A small crowd had begun to form on the sidewalk in front of the bank, calling responses to Scylla's barked chants. A few people that I recognized from the riverfront park were holding their palmtops up, recording the march. A glimmer of hope began to burn in my chest. If the group kept building like this...

Before I could even finish the thought, a black sedan with government plates turned onto Third Street, followed by three police cars. My heart sank.

Officers in riot gear leapt out of the police cars, lining the sidewalk and blockading our march. Then the passenger door to the black sedan opened, and Joseph Condor stepped onto the sidewalk. Scylla stopped dead in her tracks at the sight of him, and the rest of our demonstrators fell into an uneasy silence at the sight of the police.

Condor clapped his hands imperiously. "Right, ladies and gentlemen, I'm afraid we're going to have to put an end to this now. I'm asking you all to disperse peacefully."

"What for?" Scylla called back at him. "We're not doing anything wrong!"

"You're obstructing traffic on Third Street."

Beside me, Henry scoffed. "What traffic? This place has been deader than the cemetery."

Condor looked at him. His expression seemed to sharpen at the sight of Henry. "There have been complaints from the businesses on this street. You're causing a disturbance."

Henry squared his shoulders, meeting Condor's unspoken challenge head-on. "We have a right to freedom of speech, and we're exercising that right."

"That *privilege*," Condor corrected, "is limited by statute 15-1 of the Martian Articles of Colonization, which you are now in violation of."

"Bullshit!" Scylla snapped. "My mom helped work to pass that law during the GSAF Accords back on Earth. It was designed to prevent hate speech, not muzzle law-abiding citizens."

His gaze flashed over her. In the bright sunlight, his pupils had constricted to almost nothing. He looked like a lizard. "Hateful, seditious or dangerous speech, Miss Hwang. A court of law defines that as any speech deemed to be dangerous to the safety of Martian citizens, including that which incites a riot—"

"We're not trying to start a riot," I interrupted, my voice shaking. "We just want answers."

"And we are working on providing answers. This public display is unnecessary and is only impeding the authorities from doing their jobs. Now I'm going to ask you again to leave."

The police officers closed ranks around us. I noticed with alarm that a few of them were armed. My pulse raced. I'd never seen a real gun before—they were illegal on Mars. I didn't think the police were allowed to carry them, especially not for something as innocuous as this.

I put my hand on Henry's elbow. "Maybe we should go," I whispered.

He jerked his arm away. "No," he snapped. "I'm not backing down this time."

"Henry—"

"I'm not leaving here until you tell us where Isaak is, you slimebag," he snapped at Joseph Condor.

A police officer stepped forward, inserting himself in between Henry and Condor. "Stand down, son," he said, but Henry ignored him.

"What are you even doing here?" he shouted at Condor over the officer's head. "What does all of this have to do with you? You're just the director of land use. Why do you have so much authority?"

The crowd swelled up around me, shoving me further away from Henry. ProLibertate pushed past me, yelling, "Isn't it obvious? These statists are all alike. They get a little power and next they want it all."

Condor had disappeared behind the line of police by now.

There was no sign of him, but the anarchists didn't seem to care. Unlike me, they were ready for a riot.

"Stand *down*," the officer in the front shouted again.

"We want the truth!" someone screamed back.

I saw it happen, but I was too far away to do anything. One second I was shouting, "Henry, look out!" The next, a stream of fiery orange spray was hitting him straight in the face. The crowd erupted in screams, all the Triple-C members frantic to get out of the way of the spray without getting hit, the anarchists incensed by it. I pushed back against them, trying to get to Henry, but it was like fighting a tidal wave. I felt a hand clamp around mine, and I clutched it desperately. After a minute, I realized it was Scylla. She pulled me through the crowd, and together we managed to reach Henry, crumpled on the asphalt.

"Here, Henry, rinse your eyes." I passed him a water bottle from my messenger bag with shaking hands. Shouts rang in my ears over the pounding of my own heartbeat.

"Water's no good," Scylla said urgently, prodding my shoulder. "You need milk or something, I heard milk is good."

"Where are we supposed to get milk?!" My voice broke with hysteria. There were no grocery stores anywhere around here, and in any case, real, non-powdered milk was so expensive even my moms barely bought it.

"My bag," Henry interrupted, his voice ragged. Water was dripping from his face, running down his arms. His hair was soaked. He tried to open his eyes, then squeezed them shut again quickly.

"What?"

"There's a bottle in my bag."

66

Before I could react, Scylla had Henry's backpack open. He coughed violently and cursed under his breath as she handed him a plastic squeeze bottle.

"What is that?" I asked, washing him flush his eyes with the clear liquid.

"Dish soap and water. If that doesn't work, I've got a bottle of Maalox in there, we can mix that with your water."

I gawked at him. Scylla said, "You came prepared, didn't you?"

He looked up at her. His eyes were completely bloodshot, but at least he could keep them open now. "Well, it's a good torquing thing I did, isn't it?"

The group surrounding us was thinning. I looked around and saw that all the Triple-C kids had left. Only Henry's anarchists were left, shouting and pushing back against the officers. A few of them were being handcuffed.

"We should probably go," I said.

Henry was flushing his eyes again, but he paused and blinked up at me. "What? I'm not backing down."

"Neither are the police," I hissed under my breath. "I'm not going to stand by while they do that to you again. If you don't get out of here, they're going to arrest you. We have to leave."

"Tamara—"

"Henry."

The two of us stared at each other. I could feel Scylla watching us, but I didn't look away from him.

Finally, he sighed. "All right. I'm done for today. But I'm not giving up. I can't. Isaak—" He broke off, the unspoken words hanging in midair.

"I know." I held out my hand to help him up. "I'm not giving up, either. This isn't over."

The crowd dispersed around us, the police barking out orders and keeping everyone moving. Henry kept coughing. The sound was like an anchor against all the cacophony around us. Scylla hooked her arm around mine, drawing me toward the maglev stop. I kept Henry's hand clasped tightly in mine until we were away from the officers for fear they'd rip him away and haul him off to jail, make him disappear like Isaak. I couldn't lose him, too. I expected him to resist me, but he didn't. I glanced at him over my shoulder once and my heart sank. He looked so hopeless. So defeated.

I squeezed his fingers in what I hoped was a reassuring way. He looked up at me and managed a tight smile. I smiled back.

Defeated, but not broken. We'd be okay.

We had to be.

CHAPTER 8

- h e n r y -

I ZIPPED AND UNZIPPED MY HOODIE FOR ABOUT THE FIFTIETH time in five minutes. I hated the feeling of long sleeves on my arms, but I couldn't take it off. I'd woken up with welts up and down my arms this morning, the areas I hadn't rinsed off quickly enough yesterday. Tamara would lose her damn mind if she saw them, and I wasn't going to do that to her. So I stood here in front of my locker instead, fidgeting with my hoodie and wondering, as always, what the hell I was doing here.

The answer was always the same. Especially now. I had to make sure she was okay.

I inhaled, resting my forehead wearily against my locker door. She'd sat next to me on the train ride back to my apartment, her shoulder brushing mine. My skin still tingled with the memory. It was against the rules. Normally I would have moved away, but I'd been too torquing tired yesterday to care about the rules. I'd needed the touch to know, even if I closed my eyes against the burning air, that she wouldn't disappear into nothingness.

Maybe she'd needed that, too.

I zipped my hoodie up again and slammed the locker shut.

"Hey, Sandhu."

I started at the sound of my name, and then again when I saw who'd said it. Wyatt Ponsford. Two meters of blond asshole loomed over me.

"Ponsford," I said warily. "What's up?"

He smiled like a politician, with too many teeth. "I saw you guys on the news yesterday. Are you okay, man?"

Of course it had been on the news. Of torquing course. I should have checked Speculus last night before bed, but I'd been too busy getting nagged by parents who didn't seem to notice the fact that I didn't listen to them. I wondered what they'd say tonight. They'd have to have seen it by now. I might *have* to listen to them this time.

I kept my expression neutral. "I'm fine." I started walking toward our homeroom classroom, and, despite his longer gait, he hurried to keep up with me.

In a concerned voice, he said, "You know, Henry, when an officer tells you to stand down, if you comply with their instructions then they're less likely to use force."

And here we go. I ground my teeth. "Did I torquing ask you, Ponsford?"

"I'm just trying to help," he said, looking affronted. "I'm worried about Isaak, too, you know. But getting into it with the cops isn't going to help him."

I turned on him. "Why the hell should you be worried about Isaak?" I snapped. "You were never friends with him. If you really want to help, tell your mother to do her damn job and free him."

He blinked repeatedly at me. He looked like a malfunctioning android. Maybe that's what he actually was. Isaak would have appreciated that theory. "My mom doesn't—"

I cut him off. "Your mom is second-in-command of the whole torquing province, isn't she? So yeah. I'm pretty sure she does."

The blinking continued at an even-more-rapid pace. "You know what, Henry? I don't know why I even try with you. How you managed to become friends with Tamara is beyond me."

"It's a mystery to us all," I said. That wasn't a lie.

Wyatt made a noise of exasperation and stormed off. A moment later, I heard her voice behind me. Speak of the devil.

"There you are," Tamara said. "What did Wyatt want?"

"To be an annoying turd, which he succeeded at," I replied.

Tamara sighed disappointedly, as she did every time Isaak or I disparaged Wyatt Ponsford, but she didn't push it. "Never mind. How are you feeling?"

"I feel great," I said, falling into step beside her. "Well-rested, bright-eyed and bushy-tailed. So excited for another day of learning at this fine academic establishment."

She laughed hollowly. "Great. Me too. Just checking."

Neither of us spoke again until she turned into the classroom and stopped short. I craned my head over her and saw why.

A GSAF agent was standing at the front of the classroom.

Great. What now?

Tamara looked white as a sheet. I nudged her with my elbow, then moved past her toward Mr. Johnson. "What, so the textbook propaganda wasn't enough? You had to bring in the suits for the full effect?" It was a bad joke, but I was trying to lighten the mood before Tamara's anxiety ate her alive.

"Sorry to say it was nothing to do with me," Johnson replied. "If I'd called them, they'd be here to haul you away."

The agent was looking at me. She had a badge on the lapel of her suit jacket, GSAF's logo of a rocket soaring over Mars. A bright blue orb—Earth—winked in the distance. "You never know, you might get lucky," I said, more to myself than to Johnson.

Everyone was quiet during the announcements for once. My classmates were itching, I knew, to find out what this agent was doing here. It was probably something stupid about Career Week, I told myself hollowly. A follow-up presentation to try to lure more unsuspecting kids down the path of government bureaucracy

Right.

Mr. Aguilar signed off with his ridiculous "*Haaaaaave a nice day!*" line, and all eyes turned to Mr. Johnson.

"Hey, well," he said, somewhat stiffly under the agent's scrutiny, "as you can see, we have a visitor today. Not just us, actually. GSAF has a special presentation for the Academy, so there's one of these"—he gestured at the agent—"in every classroom. I hope you will give her your full attention."

The agent stepped forward, pressing a button on the top of the pyramidal display at the front of the classroom. "Good morning, everyone. My name is Agent Beti Klaithong. I'm here on behalf of the Global Space and Astronautics Federation, which, as I'm sure you're aware, administers the government here on Mars. We oversee the continued terraformation efforts, and more than that: we appoint the governors of each province, manage the offices of each city, take care of unincorporated land... basically, anything you can think of that needs to be done to run a planet, we do it." She smiled robotically, not unlike Wyatt Ponsford earlier. "We're responsible for the survival of the Martian colony, and we take that responsibility very seriously. We know that we're all in this together."

Her eyes fell on me, and suddenly I knew. I knew what all this was about. And my blood ran cold.

She smiled again. "Unfortunately, there have been some allegations of late that have led to some concern that GSAF may be overstepping its authority. Specifically, there was an implication stemming from students at this Academy that the government may have been involved in the disappearance of one of your classmates, a young man named Isaak Contreras. That is patently untrue, and I'm here today to explain the full story to you."

The full story. I glanced over at Tamara; she was turned around in her seat, looking at me with wide, panic-stricken eyes.

Agent Klaithong turned the pyramidal display on and expanded it so the hologram filled the whole front of the classroom. It was footage of the Kimbal dig site. I realized after a minute that it had been taken by that security drone, the one Isaak said was operated by GSAF.

They had been watching us. All along.

"As some of you may know—I understand that this class was present during the Career Week Incident"—her tone was loaded here, and a few of my classmates snickered—"Isaak was serving weekend detention at a scientific expedition run through Kimbal University. The dig was being conducted on federal land, which meant that GSAF had a security presence at the site." The screen footage showed Isaak ducking under the rope that cordoned off one of the excavation craters from the public, sliding down the side of the crater to run his hands over the stone arch that had started this whole torquing thing.

Agent Klaithong watched the hologram primly. "I'm sure most of you remember that Isaak was not exactly respectful of federal property during your field trip. Unfortunately, that behavior was not limited to just the one incident. During his weekends on the site, Isaak acquired quite the reputation for flouting procedure." The picture switched to another shot of Isaak holding a piece of metal in his gloved hand, too far away for me to make out the details. A man approached him from out of frame—Joseph Condor. I hadn't been there for this, but Isaak had told me about it. The first time Condor shut the site down.

"This series of impact craters were of great interest to some of humanity's earliest scientific expeditions to this planet, and as such, a number of robotics and satellite remnants from past missions remain in the area. Some of this technology is still considered classified, and all of it is the property of Earth's governments. As such, our contract with Kimbal University clearly stipulated that nothing was to be removed from the area, and any non-natural discoveries that the dig turned up were to be handed over to GSAF for proper cataloging."

She leaned over, tapping the pyramidal display to pause the hologram. "We had not had any prior incidents on this site before Isaak Contreras began serving there. But once he began working on the site, classified items began to disappear."

Some jackass in the back of the classroom called out, "You mean he stole them."

"Bullshit," I snapped. "They're lying."

"Sandhu," Mr. Johnson yelled from behind his desk. "I won't warn you again."

Agent Klaithong smiled. "We're not here to make judgment calls. We're just here to expose the truth." She turned the pyramidal display on again. More drone footage began playing. This time it was distant and pixelated; it was hard to make out whether it was actually Isaak in the frame or not.

"The day before Isaak Contreras disappeared, a number of disturbing finds were made at the Kimbal dig site. The most prominent of these, and the one you may have heard mentioned on the news, was the discovery of a human corpse. Tierra Nueva Police are still investigating this, but the subject is believed to be the victim of a recent homicide."

More bullshit. Isaak told us that Erick had thought the skeleton was ancient. I didn't know what it meant, but apparently GSAF was intent on keeping it that way. They were covering it up, just like everything else.

"We have reason to believe that, during the pandemonium that followed the discovery of the body, Isaak Contreras made a discovery of his own. A highly classified—and potentially dangerous—piece of equipment was stolen from the site that same day."

Bullshit the third. Whatever it was that Isaak had taken from the site, it wasn't equipment, and I seriously doubted that it was dangerous. Except for to GSAF, if it got out that they were covering up whatever had been out in those hills. I was just about to interject this—and get banished for it, I was sure—when, of all people, Wyatt Ponsford spoke up.

"But how do you know it was Isaak?" he said. "He hasn't been tried for this. He's not here to defend himself. Nobody even knows where he is. He deserves due process of the law."

She quirked her eyebrow at him. "Very legally minded, Mr...?"

"Ponsford," said Wyatt.

Recognition washed over her face. "Ah, Lieutenant Governor Ponsford's son. You take after your mother. You're right, Mr. Ponsford. But accusations have been hurled at GSAF, and we feel it's important that they be addressed. We're not pointing any fingers here; we simply want to let the truth speak for itself."

"And what is the truth?" I asked. I was getting sick of this farce.

"The truth is that Isaak Contreras is on the record as having taken something from the dig site. While his current whereabouts are still unknown, GSAF recovered his palmtop. His palmtop shows that he had plans to deliver the stolen item to a person of interest with a prior record of altercations with GSAF. And he had an accomplice."

I sucked in my breath. *Shit.*

"With the cooperation of the Academy's Campus Police and Tierra Nueva P.D., we have tracked Isaak's last known movements. This is what we discovered."

The hologram on the display switched. Now it was showing closed-circuit footage from the Academy. I recognized it as the sky bridge connecting to Tyson Hall. Isaak was leaning against the window, looking out at the bluffs. Then the door opened, and he moved to intercept someone.

No. Goddammit. Why were they bringing her into it?

On the screen, Tamara looked at Isaak in concern. There was no sound, but I could see they were talking urgently about something. And then—

She leaned in and kissed him.

I heard her—the real her, not the hologram—let out a gasp.

The floor dropped out from under me. It shouldn't have been a shock, not after all these years of bracing myself for just this sight. But it was all the same. Around us, our classmates started whooping and laughing. I wanted to tell them all to shut up, to get stuffed, but my voice wouldn't come. GSAF had no business showing this footage to other students, let alone the whole school. Tamara looked like she wanted to die. Wyatt had turned around in his seat and was saying something to her, but I couldn't hear what.

Agent Klaithong seemed pleased by the reaction. She watched with bemusement, then raised her voice to be heard over the screeching baboons around me. "This is the last known footage verifying Isaak Contreras' whereabouts. After that, he disappears... except for a few text communications with his accomplice." She folded her arms and looked at me, confirming my suspicion that she'd known all along exactly who I was. She'd been here for me. "Isn't that right, Mr. Sandhu?"

I stared at her, the room still spinning around me. "What?"

"Isaak's palmtop. He was supposed to meet you, and you were going to deliver the item to your contact together. You gave him the address, did you not?"

My mouth opened, then closed, then opened again. "Yeah, but I didn't—"

"You were the last person to have contact with Isaak Contreras. Possibly the last person to see him alive."

"No!" I exclaimed. "I didn't—"

Everyone was staring at me except Tamara. She was huddled in on herself, crying.

Mr. Johnson stood up then, slamming his hand down on the desk. That got their attention. Everyone shut up and stared at him instead of me. "All right, Agent Klaithong, that's enough. I have to insist—my students shouldn't have to go through this humiliation. I'm not going to stand here while you badger them, hurl accusations, and violate their privacy like this."

She looked at him sideways. "Well, then, if you *insist*. But please understand, Mr. Johnson. GSAF works for the people of Mars. The right to privacy only extends as far as it doesn't violate the safety of others. If it must be sacrificed for the good of the Martian people, that's a sacrifice we're prepared to make. We are only here to protect the truth."

"Right." Johnson slammed his fist on the top of the pyramidal display. It flashed and shut off. "Mission accomplished. Now please remove yourself from my classroom."

She arched her eyebrow at him. "Of course. Whatever you say." She turned to smile the class. "Have a nice day."

The classroom was silent as Agent Klaithong left. I could feel everyone's eyes on me, or Tamara, or Mr. Johnson. Wondering who was going to say something first. It wasn't going to be me. I wasn't sure my vocal cords even worked anymore.

"Look, Henry," Mr. Johnson said.

Before he could elaborate, the notifications on my deskpad started pinging. I glanced down. *Report to office.*

There wasn't a sufficient cuss word in any language for what I was feeling.

"Principal wants me," I said before anyone could say anything else. Tamara looked up at me, her face red and her eyes bloodshot.

I grabbed my backpack, but Mr. Johnson stopped me on my way out the door. He glanced at my classmates, then ushered me into the hall.

"Henry, listen," he said. "I know I always gave you a hard time, but I never..." He trailed off, looking down for a moment. "I don't believe a word of it. Whatever happens, just know that. I never wanted this to happen, and certainly not like this."

He knew what was coming. We both did.

"It's okay, Mr. J," I said. I forced a smile, and he forced one back. Maybe all these years, I'd been wrong about him.

I turned toward Tyson Hall, ready to meet the chopping block head-on.

CHAPTER 9

♫

- t a m a r a -

WE FOUND HIM DOWN BY THE BAY.

That should have been the first place I looked, honestly. That's always where Isaak used to go when he was upset. Maybe that's why I hesitated to go there at first. Why it took us hours to find him. Scylla had hurried over from Curiosity Bay when I texted her what happened, to help me look for him. It didn't help matters that he still didn't have his palmtop—GSAF never returned it, and he hadn't bought a new one yet—so we couldn't text him. I spent an agonizing two hours filled with dread that I'd never see him again, and then there he was, in the place I always knew he would be.

Gray clouds swirled in the sky over our heads, and the wind stung my cheeks as it whipped around me, dragging stray hairs into my mouth. Normally when the wind was this strong it meant rain was coming, but the air felt weirdly dry, even down here by the water.

Henry sat on a large boulder on the rocky part of the shore. I picked my way across the beach, Scylla behind me, loose pebbles making me lose my footing here and there. I stopped a short distance away from him, watching the way the breeze played at his hair, revealing his face and then obscuring it again. He didn't seem to notice us at first. He just stared out at the rolling waves while I stared at him. There was no sound apart from the wind between the rocks and the waves hitting the shore.

Then, he looked at me. My face flushed, and for an instant the only thought in my head was the image of me kissing Isaak on that security footage, and the knowledge that Henry had seen that footage, and that that shouldn't matter after everything else that happened today, but for some incomprehensible reason it mattered very much.

"I got expelled," he said finally.

"We know." I brushed my windblown hair away from my face. "Henry, we can fight this—"

He laughed humorlessly. "What's the torquing point? What good was an Academy diploma going to do me in the long run, anyway? It was always a waste of my time. It's not like I could get a job with it, not after what happened today. Now that half the province is going to think I'm a murderer."

I didn't know what to say.

Henry went back to watching the sea. After a minute, Scylla moved past me, gingerly stepping over the rocks before settling down on a boulder a few meters away from him.

We stayed there, no one speaking, for a long time.

Finally, when the sun was starting to go down, I got up on legs shaky from crouching so long and put my hand on Henry's shoulder. He started, looking up at me in surprise. I wondered if he'd forgotten I was there.

"Let's go get something to eat. How about Ivan's?" I didn't say *my treat*, though I wanted to. Isaak would have happily accepted the offer, but I knew Henry better. He had too much pride to take charity, even though that's never what I'd offered.

His mouth turned up almost imperceptibly at the corners. "Okay."

The three of us made our way up to the boardwalk, the dim twilight casting everything in shadows. On the horizon, I could just see the lights of Herschel Island twinkling on the water, reminding me that I'd skipped my music classes yet again. They were only going to let me slide for so long. But I wasn't going to think about that tonight.

Inside Ivan's Diner, it was cozy and warmly lit. The faux wood paneling on the walls evoked the feel of an old-fashioned log cabin. Set into the center of the back wall, a fire was blazing in a large stone fireplace. I caught a whiff of the burning pencil odor of the manufactured firelogs as we passed, but then a server bustled past me with a tray of pancakes and the delicious smell of maple syrup filled my nose.

Henry smirked. "You look like you feel better already."

I elbowed him. "I'm not the one we're supposed to be cheering up. Come on, can't you at least try to smile?"

He grimaced, flashing every tooth in his mouth at me. "How's that?"

I rolled my eyes. "Never mind," I said, shoving him into a booth. Scylla slid into the booth across from him, pressing herself against the window. I hesitated for a moment before taking the seat next to her. We sat there awkwardly for a while, no one talking. Scylla pretended to look at the menu. Henry stared up at the ceiling fan spinning slowly over our heads. I twisted the braided red bracelet that was still around my wrist.

Finally, Scylla sighed and shoved the menu away from herself. "So what are we going to do now? GSAF's made it clear that they're not giving this up without a fight."

"So we give them a fight," Henry said, not looking away from the ceiling fan. His voice was so flat, so completely emotionless, that I stared at him for a full minute, not sure I'd heard him right.

"You can't be serious, Henry," I sputtered. "After what they did to you today?"

He looked at me, his black eyes sparking. "I'm dead serious. They already kicked me out of school and accused me of killing my best friend. What else are they going to do?"

My mouth opened and closed wordlessly. "How can you say that? *They made Isaak disappear.* Do you want to be next?"

He shrugged. "At least then I'd know what happened to him."

"No!" I slammed my hand down on the table with a force that surprised me. Henry and Scylla both gaped at me. "No," I said again.

Scylla leaned away from me, doing some interesting things with her eyebrows. "All right, then. But we can't just do nothing. I'm not going to roll over for GSAF. Maybe we should have another protest—if we stay in the public eye, there would be more scrutiny. It's harder to make a famous person disappear."

I couldn't believe my ears. "Do you hear yourself?" I hissed. "Another torquing protest? Have you already forgotten what happened to Henry yesterday?"

"I'm fine," Henry said.

"That was just a minor setback," Scylla said eagerly. "Next time—"

"Hey, welcome to Ivan's. Are you ready to order?"

The three of us whirled on the server who'd suddenly appeared next to our table.

He shifted uncomfortably. "Or, I could just give you another minute..."

"No, it's fine," Henry said. "I want a bacon cheeseburger. With real bacon, not facon."

Scylla's eyebrows did some more things. "Hey, big spender," she muttered sardonically. "I'll have the vegan pancakes, please."

I ordered strawberry crepes, and the server left us to our awkwardness. I looked down at the frayed knot on my bracelet and sighed. "I'm going to go wash my hands before the food comes," I said, sliding out of the booth.

"Sure thing, Miss Priss," said Henry. I cuffed him across the back of his head, and he grinned, catching my eye and holding it for just a minute. I relaxed slightly at his smile. There was the normal Henry. If that side of him could just stick around a little longer, I'd feel better letting him out of my sight without fear that he would do something stupid—or dangerous.

In the bathroom, I scrubbed my hands more vigorously than was probably necessary, like I thought I could wash this day—or this week, or this month—away with soap and water. I watched the suds disappear down the drain, then glanced up at myself in the mirror. The sight of my own face made me tense; it brought back memories of seeing myself on that security footage. Everyone in the school had seen it. I didn't know why this was bothering me so much. Practically everyone I knew had paired me and Isaak off back when we were freshmen. It's not like it was a secret that he'd liked me. So why did I care if people had seen me kiss him?

I turned the water back on, splashing it on my face over and over. Wash it away. Wash it all away.

Stupid.

My hands were still dripping as I left the bathroom—I lost patience with the blow dryer. I was shaking droplets off my hands when the sound of Scylla's voice stopped me in my tracks. "Seriously, Henry, how long has this been going on?"

I paused just behind the partition separating the bathrooms from the dining room, listening.

Henry snorted. "I can't remember a time it hasn't been. As long as I've known her, I guess."

A thunk on the table made me jump. I peered cautiously around the side of the partition. Scylla had slumped over with her head in her hands. She looked up at him between splayed fingers, exasperated. I leaned back behind the partition again so she wouldn't see me. "Longer than Isaak?" I heard her ask.

Complete silence.

Scylla sighed dramatically. "Then why didn't you say anything?" Her voice was lower now. I could barely hear her. I pressed myself against the partition, straining to listen.

"Yeah, right," Henry said. "What the hell would she want with—"

"Excuse me, miss, do you need help with something?"

I turned around in horror to find our server standing just outside the partition, staring curiously at me.

"No. It's nothing," I said quickly, my cheeks burning. Between our argument at the table and me eavesdropping by the bathrooms, he must have thought I was some kind of train wreck. Face undoubtedly still red as a tomato, I hurried back to the table and slipped into the booth next to Scylla.

"I was starting to think you flushed yourself," Henry said easily. Ordinarily I would have laughed, but I was still too embarrassed, so I just gave him a wild-eyed look that probably resembled a rabid ferret.

Scylla looked back and forth between us. "Look, Henry, if you're not going to say anything—" He glared at her, and she broke off mid-sentence. Then she rolled her eyes. "Fine. Whatever. I'm not getting involved."

"What are you talking about?" I asked.

"It's nothing. Look, I need to get going, anyway." He slid out of the booth.

I jumped up after him. "What? No, you can't go!"

He chuckled. "What, are you holding me hostage?" When I didn't laugh, he sighed. "It's fine, really. I just realized that it's getting late, and I still have to think about what I'm going to say to my parents."

"Scylla and I can come with you—"

"I'm not going to disappear, Tam. I promise. I just need some alone time."

I blinked, then blinked again. "But... what about your cheeseburger?"

"Oh, right." He pulled his wallet out of his pocket and started rifling through it for cash.

"That's not what I mean," I said, reaching over and slapping the wallet closed. "I mean who's going to eat it?"

"Give it to Mama D. She likes bacon, right?" He opened the wallet again, pressing two bills into my hand. "I'll see you tomorrow—I almost said *at school*." He laughed, and my heart twisted. "Don't give me that face. It's fine. I'll still walk you to the ferry, okay?" He turned to Scylla, giving her a meaningful look while she glowered at him. "Bye, Scylla."

I stared after him as he left. As the front door swung shut, I slumped down into the booth across from Scylla. "What the hell." It felt more like a statement than a question.

Scylla sighed, resting her face on her right hand, and looked at me. "This is ridiculous."

"Tell me about it. GSAF is making people disappear, and he keeps running off by himself."

"That's not what I meant." She watched me, drumming the fingers of her left hand on the table. "Tamara, can I ask you something?"

The server had brought us all water while I'd been in the bathroom. I wasn't sure if Henry had drunk out of his, so I slid the one from my old place across the table and took a sip out of it. "Yeah, what?"

"Do you love Isaak?"

I choked on the water. Scylla watched dispassionately while I coughed, then drank more to try to drown the coughing fit. "What kind of question is that?"

"An honest one."

I stared at her. "Of course I do," I said, my voice trembling slightly. "He's my best friend."

"You know that's not how I mean it."

"Obviously," I snapped. My face was on fire. Even my torquing ears felt hot. The security footage of us on the sky bridge played over and over in my mind, and I felt a sudden fury that I should have to be so defensive about this. "Why shouldn't I like him *that* way? He's tall, he's cute, he's super nice. He's my best friend. He's had a huge crush on me for years. My moms love him. Everyone always said we were going to wind up together, that we were perfect for each other."

Scylla had stopped drumming her fingers, and now she was looking at me intently, head cocked slightly, eyes shining. "Tam," she said, her voice so earnest that it made my eyes sting inexplicably. "I'm aro. I don't even date and I know it doesn't work that way. You've got to be honest here. It's not about what other people think. Do *you* love Isaak?"

I was crying now. I couldn't even see Scylla properly anymore—her features were swimming behind the mess of my tears. Why was she asking me these questions? I didn't want to deal with this right now. There was too much going on, too much going wrong. Isaak was missing. We had to find him before it was too late. That was all that mattered. Now was not the time to think of stupid, selfish things like this.

Like the fact that that kiss had felt so, so wrong. From the minute I'd done it, I'd known it. It was over right when it should have been beginning, because it was *wrong*. All that would come out of it was a heartbroken friend or an endless lie. I should never have done it. Stupid, stupid, stupid.

Scylla slid into the booth next to me, her arms around me as I cried. I didn't even notice as the server put our food down on the table, slipping wordlessly away from us. I didn't answer her, but the unspoken word hung heavy in the air nonetheless.

No.

CHAPTER 10

- h e n r y -

I SHOULD HAVE BEEN THINKING ABOUT WHAT I WAS GOING TO tell my parents when I got home. That's what I'd said I needed to do, after all. And it was true. But instead, I spent the whole walk back to my apartment thinking about what Scylla had said at Ivan's.

She needed to butt out. But of course she wouldn't. She was like a torquing bear trap—once she'd latched onto something, she'd never let it go.

I couldn't worry about whatever stupid thing she was saying to Tamara now. If she had any human decency, she'd drop it. Tamara was worried enough about Isaak, she didn't need to worry about me on top of it. I'd be fine. I always had been. Nothing was different now.

The light was against me at the intersection across from my apartment. I pressed the pedestrian crossing button on the lamp post wistfully. No, we definitely didn't need Scylla making trouble for them. Not after those two idiots had finally stopped acting like giggling middle schoolers and gotten their damn acts together. Isaak was going to be traumatized enough once GSAF released him. The last thing we needed was for Scylla to have made drama between him and his new girlfriend on top of it. She had to understand that. She wouldn't say anything to Tamara—I had to believe that.

I was so wrapped up in my thoughts that I didn't see the figure in the shadows outside my apartment until it was too late. I tensed as he stepped forward, intercepting me at the door.

"What are you doing here?" I asked.

Joseph Condor smiled. "I just wanted to give you your palmtop back, Mr. Sandhu. It is your property, after all, and I thought you might be... let's say, *out of the loop* without it."

He held it out to me. I stared at him distrustfully for a long moment before finally reaching out to take it. He watched as I pressed my thumb to the print scanner before entering the passcode. The screen unlocked, but it didn't open to my usual home menu. Instead, a browser window was opened to a news story.

I read the headline out loud. "*Governor Brown to retire in August-II. Incoming Governor Kate Ponsford appoints Joseph Condor as her lieutenant.*" I looked up at him. "You're the new lieutenant governor?"

He shrugged with mock humility. "You seemed so concerned that a mere land use director had 'so much authority'. I just wanted to set the record straight. There's nothing I hate more than allowing false information to spread."

It was a dig. The pleasant expression on his face just turned the screws even more. He was mocking me, the way he'd been able to ruin me so easily. The way he could ruin me so much more if he felt like it, if I just gave him an excuse to do it.

I scowled at him. "Right, got it. You've made your point. But

I'm surprised that someone of your position would waste his time worrying about what a nobody like me thinks."

"You've gotten my attention, Mr. Sandhu. I'd say that in and of itself precludes you from being a mere nobody." He folded his arms. "And I trust, after today, that I've gotten your attention."

A cold breeze whistled through the open-air hallway. I shoved my palmtop into my pocket. "Yes, sir," I said sarcastically. "I've learned my place. No more trouble from Henry Sandhu. Are we done here?"

I started to turn to open the door, but he said, "No, we are not done." I sighed, pivoting back to him. "You were in contact with a man on Earth about an ancient coin that was supposedly in your possession," he said. "Who was he?"

I shrugged. "I have no clue. The fun thing about the internet is that it lets people be anonymous. That means *private identity*, in case you weren't aware."

He clucked his tongue. "Henry, Henry. You can never make it easy on yourself. The FBI tapped a man who was participating in a seditious chatspace on Earth. Sedition, in case *you* weren't aware, is a felony on Mars. So I will ask you again. Who is he, and why were you in contact with him?"

I gritted my teeth. "I don't *know*, okay? The whole thing was stupid. We were just goofing off. Can you let me through now?"

"Did you agree to sell any artifacts to him?"

"No. The coin was something Isaak's dad brought here from Earth, that's all. We were playing treasure hunt, and you can see how well that worked out for us. I don't know where it is now. I just want to forget the whole thing."

He drew close enough that I could smell the mint on his

breath. "Then forget it, Mr. Sandhu. All of it. If you stay out of our affairs, you can live your life. If you don't…" The corners of his lips turned up, just the faintest hint of a smile. "Well. Today was just the beginning."

I swallowed. "Fine. Understood."

"Good." He clapped his hand on my shoulder. "See to it that you don't forget. Because I'll know if you do."

The breeze picked up again, bringing with it the scent of spices in the air. Mom must be home, cooking dinner. I still didn't know how I was supposed to tell her that I got expelled from the Academy, let alone the protest incident or the accusations that GSAF had thrown at me. She'd kill me. If she didn't, Dad would.

I hesitated a moment, thinking about not going in. About turning and running away. I couldn't face them, not now.

In the shadows, Joseph Condor cleared his throat.

I'll know if you do.

There was nowhere else to go. I shoved my key card into the lock and opened the door.

CHAPTER 11

- t a m a r a -

A FEW WEEKS LATER, I STOOD IN THE DIMLY LIT VESTIBULE, watching people trickle through the doors of San Marcos. It was nowhere near the crowd I was used to seeing on the weekends. Most people were on their way to work at this time on a weekday, so the congregation today was mostly made up of retirees. But I hadn't seen Isaak's mom since the Saturday before the protest, and Father Alvarez commented that she was coming to Mass during the week now.

I needed to talk to her. I'd had to wait until school got out for the off-term, but I was finally here. She had to come.

Just before eight, she appeared through the side door, wearing the same black pantsuit she'd had on the last time I saw her. Celeste wasn't with her—maybe Erick was watching her now, since he was nowhere to be seen, either.

I watched her for a moment, my heart aching at the sight of her. She'd lost a lot of weight, deep creases carved into a face where there had once been just the faintest of laugh lines.

"Dr. Garcia," I said, moving to approach her.

She stopped short, her face inexplicably wary. "Tamara."

Her reaction stymied me. Awkwardly, I said, "I was hoping I'd run into you. I've been trying to get a hold of you for a few weeks now. I don't know if you got my message, but I was wondering if you and Erick and Celeste might be interested in being my guests at the museum opening next week." The board of directors had asked me to compose some original music to play during the gala. Isaak had been supposed to go with me as my... date. I tried not to dwell on that. Every time I did, my eyes started prickling and my throat squeezed closed. I wasn't going to think about any of that anymore. What mattered was that I still wanted Isaak's family to come. He'd been really excited about this museum opening—there was even going to be an exhibit on Olmec archaeology, featuring some of his grandfather's work. I wanted them to see it, even if he couldn't.

Dr. Garcia shifted from foot to foot, looking down at her shoes for a moment. "Yeah, I did get your message. But I don't think we'll be able to go. I'm sorry."

I tried not to let my face fall visibly. "That's okay. Maybe some other time?"

"Maybe." She glanced in my direction, but it was like she didn't quite see me—she was looking past me, or through me.

"What about the Earth Vibes Festival at the waterfront next month? They're going to have dragon boats, Celeste might like that."

"I don't think so." Her lips formed a tight line. "Listen, Tamara... Honestly, we're going through a lot right now. We're trying to focus on getting through this as a family, for Celeste's sake. We don't need a reminder..." She trailed off, then changed gears. "What I'm trying to say is, whatever he did, Isaak had clearly lost his way. The people in his life led him astray. I don't want the rest of my family following him."

Her voice had turned cold. I stared at her, my brain struggling to process what she was saying. Then it dawned, with sudden clarity. She'd seen the video. GSAF had shown her the video. And now she blamed me.

Why was it so easy for them to ruin everything?

I swallowed hard. "I understand how you feel," I said in the smallest of voices.

A cordial smile. "Good. Then you'll understand that I'd appreciate it if you didn't try to reach out to us again."

I nodded, trying to seem nonchalant. "Of course. I only want what's best for you guys."

She smiled again, a bit more genuinely this time, and I remembered all the times I'd played over at their house when I was little, and the three of us—Henry, Isaak and me—helping her in the garden, and her and Isaak and Celeste sitting in the front row at my last piano recital. It wasn't enough that GSAF had taken my best friend from me, now I was losing my second family and there was nothing I could do about it.

She dipped her fingers into the font of holy water and crossed herself, stepping from the vestibule into the church. I watched her go, but didn't move to follow her. The line had been drawn. I wasn't welcome.

I blessed myself, glancing back over my shoulder before I left the cathedral.

"Goodbye," I whispered.

SUMMER

2073 C.E.

CHAPTER 12

- h e n r y -

THE NEXT SEVERAL MONTHS WENT BY IN A BLUR. TO SAY MY parents had been displeased about me getting expelled—on top of everything else—would be an understatement. A lot of things had come to an end that day. My relationship with my mom and dad was just one of them.

I'd spent most of June-II looking for a job and a place to live. I had enough money saved up from my freelance jobs for a deposit, at least, but there was no way I would have made rent on just that. So I started working in the factory district, at a manufacturing plant that made parts for AresTec.

I didn't tell Tamara. She would have just worried more, or tried to get her moms to use their influence to get me something better. Neither of us needed that. So I just told her I was working *somewhere* and changed the subject whenever she pressed. And when she'd ask if I'd enrolled at South Tierra Nueva High for next annum, I'd just smile and nod and, when necessary, flat-out lie about it. Hell no, I wasn't going to South. What good, exactly, would a diploma from there have done me? None. I wasn't wasting any more time in state-sanctioned indoctrination camps.

I had something more important to work on.

Scylla, on the other hand, hadn't given up on her little pep rally daydreams. After the incident downtown, she'd switched tactics. A conversation with one of her professors revealed that the Kimbal University campus was one of GSAF's designated free speech zones, so she decided to try to ramp up interest among her classmates. Of all people, she'd kept in touch with ProLibertate, that jerk from Speculus who'd helped turn her first protest into a true shitshow. They were trying to start a hashtag movement. It was slow going, what with Grant squawking at every turn about what rabble-rousers we'd all been on site, but she at least got some interest from some poli-sci students who were writing their theses on government transparency. Snort.

One time, I started to tell her that what she was doing wasn't going to help Isaak, but she cut me off. She looked at me with a funny expression, one I'd never seen on Scylla's face before. It took me a minute to realize that she was on the verge of tears.

"I have to do *something*," she hissed, her nose red and her voice wobbling.

I kept my mouth shut after that. It didn't matter, anyway. Her little protests were a good distraction. As long as she kept that up, hopefully GSAF wouldn't notice what I was really up to.

As for Tamara... well, she wasn't around too much after June. She'd finally gotten her big break—at the museum gala, of all places. Scylla and I wound up going that night, to support her. I had a fairly miserable time. I mean, the museum was really fresh and everything, and Tamara's new songs were stellar, but the guilt of knowing that Isaak was the one who was supposed to be there with her was crushing. I spent the night in a fog, Scylla prodding me periodically with the toothpick umbrella out of her drink—she'd lorded over me all night that she was old enough to order from the bar and I wasn't—and telling me to *snap out of it.* We were there for Tamara.

As if I'd needed reminding. In case Scylla hadn't noticed (which she definitely had), it was practically impossible for me to keep my mind on anything else when Tamara was around.

But as it turned out, Tamara hadn't had much time to talk to either of us, anyway. One of the guests at the gala just happened to be a music producer from Earth, and he was interested in Tamara's talent. Very interested. He'd swept her off to go introduce her to some of his contacts, leaving Scylla and me standing there awkwardly making small talk with the few museum donors who were willing to be seen with a long-haired Indian kid in a hand-me-down suit and sneakers and an increasingly tipsy Korean vegan.

By the end of the evening, Tamara had an offer for a recording contract on Earth. She didn't take it just then; she told the guy that she wanted to finish high school first, which just killed me. Tamara was another person that really didn't need the Academy to get where she was going. She had the talent on her own. But she wanted to go to the Herschel Institute after high school. She'd been working for it for years with her pre-college classes there. The Herschel Institute was on par with Juilliard, as she'd told me a bajillion times before, and to go there, she had to have her diploma. So she was staying a while longer. But she was busy nonstop during the whole off-term, taking extra lessons at Herschel and workshops from all these pros that producer hooked her up with. Between that and my erratic hours at the factory, it seemed like I never saw her anymore, even though she

101

texted almost every day.

Sometimes it felt like all those easy years of the three of us together, Isaak, Tamara and me, had been a dream. Or maybe the real truth was that Tamara and I were like the moons, Phobos and Deimos—traveling at different speeds, in different directions. The only thing that had kept us together was the gravity of Isaak, and now that gravity was gone. Without that planet's pull, what was to keep us from drifting off into space?

We lived in different worlds. I'd always known it, but those months proved it.

I sighed as I leaned against the slick metal railing of the pier, swatting a bug away from my face. In odd-years, October fell directly in the middle of summer, and it definitely felt like it this year. It was hotter than I ever remembered it being, and it hadn't rained yet this season, which was unusual. It hadn't rained since spring. But the insects—the one Earth transplant that hadn't seemed to have any difficulty adapting to life on another planet—didn't seem to mind. They thrived in the heat. They'd been terrible this summer.

A squealing group of kids in costumes raced past me, brandishing plastic jack o'lanterns. That was at least the tenth group that had gone by since I got here. The city was holding some kind of "safe" trick-or-treating event on the boardwalk tonight, for all the parents who didn't trust other adults enough to let their kids go around the neighborhoods. I watched a little girl in a superhero costume for a minute, resisting the urge to smile. When I was a kid, this time of year had always been an awkward juggling act between Diwali and Halloween, with me hoping that my family's holiday wouldn't interfere with trick-or-treating.

But now it didn't seem to matter. I didn't associate the end of October with lighting candles or with panhandling for candy anymore. This day was only ever going to be one thing for me now.

Isaak's birthday.

I jammed my hands in my pockets, breathing in the briny scent of the water behind me and remembering. Last year he'd been complaining that his mom was making him take Celeste out because she had to work late, even though he and I had planned an all-night horror flick marathon. I wondered who would take Celeste trick-or-treating this year.

The fluorescent lights overhead started flipping on around me as the sky grew darker. Each lamppost had black-and-orange streamers hanging from it, with a banner of a jack o'lantern here, a sugar skull there. It felt festive and cheery, but I couldn't stop staring at the one with the skull. Its lipless grin seemed to be mocking me.

"Henry."

I turned at the sound of her voice only to see another painted skull leering at me across the dock. The figure was shrouded in a wispy greenish-gray material that streamed out around her, trailing behind her like an eerie fog. Green hair framed her face like clumps of seaweed.

"What are you supposed to be, the Grim Reaper?" I asked.

Tamara grinned, breaking the effect of the painted-on teeth. "I'm a banshee calavera," she said, glancing down at herself. "My moms had their annual argument over whose culture I should rep, so I gave up and decided to compromise. Do you think I look stupid?"

I wanted to say, *You would never look stupid*. Instead, I said, "No stupider than anyone else tonight."

She jabbed me in the ribs, and the two of us laughed. I'd missed that sound.

Then her smile faded, and she stepped closer, holding out a white cardboard box. "I'm ready if you are," she said, her voice barely above a whisper.

I inhaled and nodded. "As much as I'll ever be."

We made our way down to the beach, stepping gingerly over loose rocks in the silty red sand. Tamara gestured to me, looking disconcertingly like a mythical harbinger of doom, and I followed her away from the lighted pier. She led me to a secluded cove, almost untouched by the lights from the city. The water looked black, but the sky was full of stars. I looked around and nodded. This was a good place.

She looked around the cove herself before turning and opening the white box, holding it out for me to see. There was a single cupcake inside, from one of those kitschy bakeries on the boardwalk that the tourists loved. A spiral of dark buttercream frosting was dotted with sugary orange-and-black sprinkles, and a small unlit candle protruded from its center.

"I got him chocolate," she said.

"Good job," I replied. I pulled a plastic lighter out of my pocket. "He probably would have disowned you if it had been vanilla."

She smiled softly as I cupped my left hand over hers to brace the box and lit the candle with my right. It flickered, casting an orange glow across her painted face. I watched her just a moment longer than necessary before dropping my hands.

"Right," she said, swallowing. "Here we go."

As she moved toward the water's edge, a soft breeze picked up, making the gauzy streamers of her skirt dance. I followed her, a few steps behind as she kicked off her sandals and waded into the shallows. As the waves lapped around her ankles, she crouched and tenderly placed the cardboard box, candle still lit, into the water. It surged forward, then bobbed back, pulled further into the bay with the ebb and flow of the tide.

She glanced at me and nodded. I closed my eyes and took a deep breath.

"Happy birthday to you..."

My voice was shaking, but Tamara's was strong enough to carry it—and keep me in key. I watched as the little makeshift boat made its way across the water. I was certain that the first good wave would completely submerge it, or bring it right back to us, but to my surprise, it bobbed over the top and kept drifting further out undaunted. Up and down, back and forth, the tiny pinprick of light growing smaller, flickering but never going out. Then, finally, it disappeared into the bay.

Tamara and I were alone.

Chapter 13

♫

- t a m a r a -

A MONTH LATER, THE HEAT WAVE WE'D HAD IN OCTOBER HAD already started to recede, even though autumn was still a few months off. This October had seen the hottest recorded temperatures on Mars, and everyone had celebrated how far terraformation had come. But now we were back to fifteen centigrade on a daily basis, and I was wondering if maybe everyone had celebrated too soon.

A cold breeze off the bay slapped me in the face as I turned to Scylla. She laughed, pulling my fallen jacket hood back up over my head. When her hand moved away, I noticed that she was wearing a new red bracelet, this one thicker and braided with a more intricate pattern than the one she'd given me all those months ago. "Sorry, what was that?" she asked.

"I said I want to look at the paddle steamer next," I repeated. "Is that okay?"

Before she could respond, Henry snorted. "Whatever you want. You're the one who wanted to come here."

I frowned. "If you didn't want to come, you could have said something."

He glanced at me. "It's your birthday, Tam," he said. "You call the shots."

I pursed my lips. We were at the Port of Tierra Nueva's Boats of the World show. They'd brought in replicas of all sorts of ships from Earth's history, from Egyptian barques to three-masted schooners. We'd just finished touring a working pirate ship replica. It was fresh and everything, but honestly, I'd only suggested coming here because I wanted *something* to do. It felt like such a struggle to bring the three of us together anymore these days. My birthday made a good excuse for it, and this at least was free and centrally located.

I missed the days when things had been easier. When we didn't have to schedule get-togethers, we just... were. Scylla was one thing, but Henry had been so weird the last several months. He was keeping secrets, I could tell. I knew part of it was that he didn't want me to know where he was working—I'd figured out that it was somewhere in the factory district, but he wouldn't talk to me about it—but it was more than that. He was up to something, and that worried me. Now that he was living on his own, he didn't have a lifeline. Scylla had her college friends, I had my friends from the Academy and Herschel, but Henry had pushed everyone else away. I wasn't ready to lose him, even if he seemed determined to lose himself.

The inside of the boat was warmer—stuffy, even. I pulled off my jacket and tied the arms around my waist. We wandered the engine room and the firebox of the paddle boat, me half reading the informational plaques below the various working parts, half watching Henry as if to make sure he didn't disappear.

"Look at this thing," Scylla said, pointing up at the enormous boiler. A brass pressure gauge was mounted next to some kind of old-fashioned speedometer. Though the boat wasn't running, the needle pointed to *ahead full*. "Let's take a holo in front of it."

I slid my palmtop out of my jeans pocket, looking around for someone to take the picture for us.

"I can take it," said Henry.

"No, I want you to be in it, too," I said. "Look, here comes a group. Excuse me, could you—?" I broke off when I recognized the blond boy who'd just come down the stairs with a group of guys from the Academy's student council. "Wyatt!"

"Oh, hey, Tamara." He looked past me into the depths of the firebox where my friends stood. Scylla smiled. Henry scowled. "Sandhu! Long time, no see, man. How are you doing? How's South?"

"Fine," Henry said stonily, turning back to the boiler and running a hand over the pressure gauge. I hooked my fingers around the belt loops on my jeans and looked down at my shoes, my lips pressed tightly together. I knew Henry wasn't going to school anymore. Just another thing he was trying to hide from me.

The student council guys glanced at Wyatt, then each other, before detaching themselves and making a production of studying the enormous steam line suspended above our heads. Scylla flitted over to Wyatt like the social butterfly she was, sticking her hand out to shake his and grinning. "Hey, I'm Scylla," she said. "And I know you. Wyatt Ponsford. You're the new governor's kid, right?"

Wyatt's ears turned bright red. "Yeah, I guess." He turned to me, eager to change the subject. "Speaking of which, my mom wanted to know if we were still on for New Year's."

Out of the corner of my eye, I saw Henry turn his head toward us, listening but trying to look like he wasn't. "I'm still thinking about it," I said awkwardly.

"What's this, now?" Scylla lifted her eyebrows and looked between us with interest.

I sighed. "Wyatt's mom wanted me to be part of the entertainment at her New Year's party."

Her mouth opened wide, shifting from a large O to a broad grin. "Fresh, Tam! The governor's New Year's bash is the biggest event in the province! You should totally do it."

"Yeah, I'm thinking about it."

I glanced over at Henry again surreptitiously—or so I thought, until Wyatt followed my gaze and grinned. "You guys should come, too. The more the merrier, and maybe Tamara's feet will be a bit less cold with more friends there."

Scylla squealed. "A New Year's party at the governor's mansion? Count me in!"

"The governor?" Henry knocked his hand against the boiler and listened to the hollow echo of metal. "I didn't vote for her." He turned his head toward us, the curtain of his hair obscuring half his face. "Oh, that's right. We don't have free elections on Mars."

Wyatt looked crestfallen. I rolled my eyes and marched over to him. "Come on, Henry," I said in a low voice. "You can get off your soapbox for five torquing minutes. It's really nice of Wyatt to invite you guys."

He muttered, "You're seriously going to go to a party held by a government official appointed by GSAF? After everything that's happened this year?"

109

I gnawed on my lip. "Not everyone at GSAF was involved with that. Isaak's mom works for them too, remember?" He stared past me, not saying anything. "Besides," I went on, "Wyatt has always stood up for you. He's a decent guy. Can't you at least *try* to make an effort?"

He sighed and ran a hand through his hair. "Fine." In a louder voice, he called, "All right, Ponsford, I'll come to your little New Year's shindig."

Scylla squealed, clapping her hands, and Wyatt grinned. "Really? Stellar. I'll forward you guys the invitation."

As Scylla excitedly rattled off her palmtop address, Henry started to turn away, but I stayed him.

"Henry," I said, "thank you."

He nudged my arm, his knuckles brushing the skin where the sleeve of my t-shirt cut off, just before my elbow. "No biggie," he said, even though we both knew it was.

Wyatt rejoined the student council guys, and the three of us moved out of the firebox, holo-snap forgotten. I absentmindedly curled my fingers around my left elbow, holding in the warmth of Henry's touch just a little longer.

CHAPTER 14

- h e n r y -

I FUMBLED WITH THE BUTTONS ON MY SHIRT IN FRUSTRATION. My fingers were itching to be behind a keyboard again, and that need made them clumsy. The thought of wasting tonight on Ponsford's New Year's party was about as appealing as a steaming hot mug of cyanide. I hardly had any free time these days with all my hours at the factory, and what time I did have was supposed to be spent on my *project*. I had to remind myself that this was technically part of my project, too—providing I could pull it off.

I paused on the last button, frowning. Tamara would be furious if she knew what I was doing. It was incredibly dangerous, hacking into GSAF's network like this. Especially after what Joseph Condor had said about them watching me. But I was relatively confident I could pull it off. After all, they hadn't seemed to have detected any of my breaches so far.

They'd been small hacks at first, just sending out feelers to see if I could learn anything about Isaak. But all I'd found after six months of trying were more questions. I could barely find anything about Isaak, and when I tried to probe Erick's former dig site, I hit a wall. But what I did keep coming across, in multitudes, was correspondence with GalaX—AresTec's parent company—

loaded with cryptic references to some kind of technology they were working on.

I didn't like it one bit. I kept remembering Scylla's artifact, the one that had disappeared along with Isaak. The one that had Mama D's maker mark on it. She said she'd never seen it before, but she worked for AresTec, and she'd been with GalaX for years before that. I was sure she wouldn't have lied to us, but that didn't mean there wasn't a connection she didn't know about. How much access did they have to her equipment, her designs?

I needed to get in deeper to find out what was really going on. And that meant getting closer to GSAF's higher-ups. This invite from Ponsford was basically a gift from the gods, and I wasn't going to squander the opportunity to get up close to the servers in the governor's mansion.

The only problem was that this was risky. The riskiest thing I'd done since I'd gotten expelled. Remote hacks were one thing, but if they detected a breach from inside on a night when I was known to be there... Let's just say, it was more important than ever to not get caught.

I straightened my tie and glanced in the mirror. My reflection made me glower. I looked ridiculous. I hated ties. The only times I'd worn them before were for my interview with the scholarship board at the Academy and freshman year when Isaak talked me into going to winter formal with him and Tamara—to make it seem less like a date, even though both of them wanted it to be one and everyone knew it.

I wasn't going to think of that tonight, I decided, turning away from the mirror. I had too many other things on my mind, more important things. I pulled my shoes on and started for the door, but as I reached for the handle, a knock made me freeze.

I thought for a second I'd misheard it, but then it came again, and I heard voices from the other side. I drew in a breath. No one ever came here to see me. My parents still weren't speaking to me. I was meeting Tamara and Scylla at Ponsford's house, and a quick glance at my palmtop showed that neither had texted with a change of plans. There was only one person that I could imagine showing up at my apartment, and he was the last person on Mars I wanted to see.

Another knock, and then a man's voice called out, "Henry Sandhu? Open up, we know you're inside."

Goddammit. I closed my eyes, summoning up all my inner strength. Then I flung the door open.

"Well, well, don't you look nice?" Joseph Condor said with a smirk. Behind him, two suited goons watched me expressionlessly. "Going somewhere special?"

"As a matter of fact, I am. And I'm going to be late if I don't leave in the next few minutes, so forgive me if I don't invite you in."

"Oh, this won't take more than a few minutes—depending on how cooperative you are." He smiled at me, all civility. "But I'm afraid it won't do for us to chat in the hall. This matter is a bit... well, confidential."

I gritted my teeth. "Well, it's going to have to wait, Mr. Condor. Because I need to leave."

"Come now, Henry. Matters of interplanetary security have to take precedent over insignificant little parties."

"How did you—" I started, but I broke off when I realized *of course* he knew where I was going. He was the lieutenant governor now. He'd probably been invited to the party himself, and I'd almost blundered right into his path. How could I have been so careless? I tried to shrug it off, seem as clueless as possible. "Matters of interplanetary security don't have much to do with me."

"Your extracurricular activities indicate otherwise." He folded his arms. "It's obvious that I haven't made an impact on you, Henry. All the warnings I've given you to leave well enough alone. Apparently you don't care about the consequences for yourself. But, you know, reckless behavior can leave collateral damage. It would be unfortunate if anyone else got hurt because of you." He smiled again as the breath left my body completely. "As I said—you were just inviting us in, right?"

I inhaled shakily and stepped back. Condor and the two men came in, and I closed the door behind them.

CHAPTER 15

- t a m a r a -

I'D NEVER EXPECTED SO MANY PEOPLE TO BE HERE. IF I'D KNOWN, I don't think I ever would have agreed to this. Even though Scylla had called it the biggest event in the province, I guess I was expecting something on the level of the museum opening, which had mostly comprised of wealthy art patrons and an assorted handful of AresTec or GSAF higher-ups. I swear, half of Mars was here tonight. There were hundreds of people crammed into Wyatt's new backyard. A tall stage was erected facing the patio, ideally placed for everyone to watch me sing, guaranteed to give them a perfect view if I screwed up.

My heart was beating firmly in my throat, and refused to get back down into my chest.

"There's nothing to worry about, love," Mama said, rubbing her hand across my back. "You'll be grand."

I smiled weakly and glanced around to see if Henry had appeared yet. I had rooted myself under a large patio heater, with a clear view of both the doors to the house and the gate where security guards were letting people with invitations through. I shouldn't have missed him, but I couldn't believe how late he was. I slipped my palmtop out of my purse to see if he'd texted.

Nothing.

"Delia, there you are." A woman with silvery hair in a chic, blunt-edged bob glided over to us. "I was hoping I'd run into you tonight. I wanted to ask you if there's been any progress on the Rainier acquisition."

"Ah, Bryn's heading that project up," Mama said. "She's here somewhere... Tamara, love, do you mind?"

I shook my head and Mama winked at me before leading the woman across the patio to where Mom had disappeared into the crowd earlier. I took an anxious sip of fruit punch that had gone watery with melted ice cubes. It was just as well—I wasn't going to be good company tonight, at least not until this performance was over. Scylla had figured that out early on and drifted off with Wyatt and Shauna. I sighed, looking up at the flickering flames in the heater over my head, and wondered if this was ever going to get better. I'd been giving recitals since I was a little kid, but I could never seem to escape the overpowering wave of anxiety that came before I performed in public. How was I ever supposed to be a professional musician if I had a panic attack any time I did anything like this?

I closed my eyes and inhaled. *Just take it one step at a time*, I told myself, repeating the advice everyone from my moms to my music teachers had always given me. *One breath. One beat. One note. It's okay to feel this way, as long as you don't let it stop you.*

"Tamara," a man's voice said. My eyes flew open, hoping for just an instant that it was Henry, but I realized just as my gaze fell on him that this voice was too high and nasal. It was Adam Harris, the music producer I'd worked with over the off-term. "I was hoping to run into you here. I'm looking forward to your performance tonight. I thought you said you weren't interested in doing anything professional until after you graduated."

My face flushed. "This isn't professional. I'm just doing it because the Ponsfords are family friends."

"Of course, of course." He folded his arms, looking over at the stage quietly for a moment. "My offer is still open, though. When you're done at the Academy, we want you at Griffin Records. Mr. Park has been in touch with Herschel, and they're willing to work your schedule around it."

I raised my eyebrows in surprise. I hadn't realized Adam was this invested in me. If the president of his label had been in touch with Herschel, they must really mean business. Suddenly I felt even more pressure to not screw up. "Thanks," I said softly.

"Just keep it in mind. I'll be watching you tonight."

He moved away from me. My eyes followed him, my stomach twisting as he attached himself to another group across the patio. *I'll be watching you.* For some reason, his words reminded me of GSAF, and my mind darted to Henry. Even when there was no reason to be alarmed—even though it had been months since our last run-in with Joseph Condor—I always worried whenever I couldn't get a hold of him. I looked at my palmtop again. Where was he?

Now I had two things to be worried about tonight.

"There you are," Wyatt said, appearing out of nowhere next to me beneath the heat lamp. "Mom was asking about you. They need you backstage. The band is starting to set up."

I gulped down my punch. "That time already, huh?"

"Don't look so worried. Everyone's looking forward to it. Just enjoy yourself."

117

Enjoy myself. He was right. I liked—*loved*—singing. That's what I needed to focus on. I nodded and stammered out some sort of reply to Wyatt, walking away from him and toward the stage.

I slowed my steps, watching the band members talking to each other as the sound crew ran back and forth, glancing at their palmtops and clutching their earpieces, struggling to communicate over the cacophony of the crowd. Most of the equipment had already been set up, which made the impending concert all the more real.

The guitarist lifted her head and smiled curiously at me, waving me over. She was probably wondering what I was doing just lurking there awkwardly rather than coming over and introducing myself. I took a deep breath and tried to smile as naturally as I could manage, walking up to her.

"Well, there's our star on the rise," she said, rising to her feet. She stuck out her hand to me, her wrist jangling with a variety of bracelets. "I'm Aya."

I offered her my own hand. "Hi, nice to meet you. I'm Tamara." Aya looked like she was in her thirties. I glanced around and noticed that the other band members, too, were quite a bit older than I was. I even recognized the drummer from a band I'd liked when I was growing up. *They hired professionals. Of course.* That didn't put the pressure on at all.

Aya smiled warmly at me. "Let's get you introduced to the rest of the gang, and then we can sound check." She turned her head and practically barked, "Hey, guys!"

The drummer and bass guitarist both paused in their actions and came over to us.

"Guys, this is Tamara. Tamara, this is Rory"—she indicated the drummer, a muscular man with short cropped blond hair—"and Craig." A man with dreadlocks pulled into a short ponytail grinned at me, his guitar strapped to his back.

Swallowing the knot in my throat, I lifted my hand. "Hi, it's nice to meet you. I'm—I'm honored to be working with you guys."

Rory and Craig smiled good-naturedly. "I'm going to go out on a limb here and guess that this is one of your first gigs," Craig surmised.

I felt my cheeks redden and nodded, feeling like such a greenhorn. "Yeah."

"I'm going to give you the best piece of advice I can: make sure your equipment is in tip-top shape, and then just forget everything and have *fun*," Aya said, her brown eyes sparkling.

"Okay," I squeaked, the word coming out sounding more like a question than I'd meant it to. Aya called over the sound engineer, and she guided me to the keyboard they'd set up for me. It was in the middle of the stage, in front of the drums. I realized with a racing heart that I would be front and center, all eyes on me.

"Everything should be good to go, but we'll do some tests. Is that a good height for you?" the sound engineer asked, indicating the microphone.

I gripped the microphone in its stand and nodded. My fingers itched to reach into my pocket and check my palmtop for a text from Henry, but I resisted. My stomach twisting in knots was just from the concert, nothing else.

My nerves settled while we did the sound checks, as I became so focused on the tuning of the keys that everything else flew from my mind.

"Five minutes to show time," the stage manager said as he walked past us.

The butterflies began to take flight again. I glanced around at the band. Aya caught my eye and winked. I smiled back, though it felt a bit wobbly. I stared out at the sea of people. Everyone's features blurred together; for an instant, I thought I saw Scylla waving at me, but then the lighting crew adjusted the spotlights and Wyatt's backyard was cast in an undefined glow of ethereal jewel tones.

He'll be here, I told myself. *There's nothing to worry about. He's probably here already.*

The lights went dark for a minute, indicating that the concert was starting. I exhaled slowly and relaxed my wrists, my yarn bracelet sliding down it as I did so. The touch of it grounded me. Thinking about Isaak made me remember the night I'd played him my music. It still hurt, when it should have been a pleasant memory. He'd genuinely liked listening to me sing. It had taken his mind off of our troubles, if even for a few minutes.

That's what I loved about music. It had the power to make your worries disappear. When you were caught in a melody, nothing else mattered.

I closed my eyes for the briefest of moments, trying to shut out all of the bad memories—Isaak—his disappearance—Henry—Joseph Condor—all of it. Focus on the music. For me. For my friends.

My fingers maneuvered across the keys, playing the intro to my song. I added my voice, noticing vaguely in the background that people began cheering my name. My heart raced as the chords from the guitars and the beat of the drum joined in. By the refrain, I found myself grinning from ear to ear. Aya, Craig, and Rory were professional, all right—and they made *me* sound professional, too.

The audience started to clap to the refrain, perfectly in rhythm. My bandmates laughed, and I found myself laughing, too. My head—and my heart—had never felt lighter when performing in front of people. Music was a kind of magic, and I found my fingertips tingling as they danced across the keys.

When I'd played the last note of the final song of the set, I found my heart sinking. I hadn't realized how high on cloud nine I was until it was over. I smiled and took the microphone in my hands. "Wow, guys," I said breathlessly, my voice booming over the speakers in Wyatt's backyard. "Thank you so much, you've been an amazing audience. I'd like to thank the Ponsfords for inviting me to perform, the lights and sound crew, and lastly, the band." I turned around to see Aya, Rory, and Craig grin and wave to the cheering audience.

I was about to step away from the microphone when I heard the crowd chanting, "Encore! Encore!"

Instead of feeling nervous, I felt relieved, glancing at the band to get their okay. I stepped up to the keyboard and began to play one last song for the night, reveling in the audience's clapping. Being onstage, feeling the crowd's energy, was an amazing rush that I found myself thriving on.

All too soon, the lights dimmed, and the concert hall was transformed back into Wyatt's backyard. I stepped away from the keyboard, feeling happy and yet disappointed that it had to come to an end.

Aya came over and hugged me. "You did *fantastic*, honey," she told me, tucking a strand of long dark hair behind her ear. "I think Tamara Randall-Torres is going to be a name we'll be seeing in lights very soon."

I smiled shyly, opening my mouth to reply.

"Tamara!" I turned my head to see Adam Harris had joined us on the stage.

Aya raised her eyebrows with a smile that clearly said, "I told you so." She patted my arm and left.

Before Adam could even open his mouth, I blurted out, "Yes!"

He laughed incredulously. "I haven't even said anything yet."

I blushed at my outburst. "Sorry, I'm just…"

"Reveling in the moment?" Adam asked with a knowing chuckle.

I bit my lip and nodded, trying to calm my racing heart. "Yeah. What I mean is, yes, I would love to sign with Griffin Records. That is," I stammered, worried I'd jumped the gun, "if the offer is…"

"Still open?" Adam asked. He smiled. "I haven't changed my mind in the past couple hours—except that you're even better than I thought. Griffin Records is going to do big things for you, Tamara, just wait and see."

I grinned. "Thank you, Mr. Harris," I said, shaking his hand enthusiastically. I watched as he walked away, before exiting the stage steps myself.

Instantly, I was bombarded. "Tamara!" Scylla squealed, flinging her arms around me. "You were stellar! That was so fresh—the freshest—I don't even have words!"

I laughed, hugging her back. "I'm so glad you liked it!"

She released me, and I glanced over her shoulder, still half expecting to see Henry lingering just behind her. But she was alone.

"Henry's not with you?" I asked, worry slamming me like a tidal wave, wiping out all the remaining joy the concert had left me with.

"No, I haven't seen him tonight," Scylla said, her brows furrowed. "He hasn't texted you?"

I ripped my palmtop out of my bag. Nothing.

Oh my God. Where was he?

"I'm sure it's nothing," Scylla said, quickly checking her own palmtop. "You know how he is. He probably couldn't bring himself to show up at GSAF Central. I'm sure he's back at his apartment, sulking about representational government. And you know service is always terrible on New Year's. Everyone's blowing each other's palmtops up. He'll probably get all our texts in a dump tomorrow afternoon."

"Yeah," I said hollowly. Up on the stage, a cleanup crew was quickly replacing the concert setup with a replica of the New Year's Ball from New York City. Midnight was just around the corner. Part of me was itching to leave now, hurry over to Henry's apartment just to check on him and make sure he was okay. But if I left now, people would notice. My moms would worry.

I swallowed, shoving my palmtop back into my purse. I'd wait until midnight. And if he wasn't here by then—I'd go check.

He was fine. Everything was fine. There was no need to panic.

For some reason, I just didn't believe it.

✦

Midnight came and went, the crowd gleefully cheering as the ball dropped, my moms kissing each other and then me. I checked my palmtop frantically, but though group messages from classmates wishing each other *Happy New Year* chimed in every few seconds, there was still nothing from Henry.

At 12:30, I crept away from the party, hoping no one would notice my disappearance. I knew I was being ridiculous. I just needed to make sure.

I'd only been to his new apartment a few times—Henry was nothing if not proud, and his place wasn't exactly in the best part of town. It seemed particularly gray and dingy tonight, with most of the lights in the building turned off. Everybody must have been out, celebrating the new year somewhere more cheerful than here.

In front of Henry's door, I paused, taking a deep breath to steady myself. Then I reached up to knock on the door—and froze, horrified.

The doorknob was unlatched. The door to his apartment was open.

Something had happened, I knew it.

"Henry?" I said, my voice barely louder than a whisper. I pushed the door open slightly and looked in. The apartment was dark, seemingly abandoned. My heart pounded in my ears as I opened the door the rest of the way and flicked the light switch on.

The apartment was a wreck. What little furniture Henry had was upended and destroyed. His air mattress was slashed, and the green papasan—the one decent chair he owned—looked like someone had put their foot through the seat. Broken wood splintered out in two different directions. I looked around the room, feeling numb, and caught a glimpse of the plain glass mirror on the wall. It was shattered. Trickles of red smeared across it. Blood.

I gasped, hurrying into the apartment, the door swinging shut behind me. "Henry?" I called out again, louder this time. No response came, but I tripped over a foot as I passed the ruined papasan and nearly screamed.

Henry sat on the floor behind the chair, his back against the wall. I thought for a moment he was unconscious—I didn't dare think what else he could be—but I realized after a moment that his eyes were open. He was holding a tie in his hands, and he stared at it glassily through the thick curtain of his long hair. His right knuckles were bloody, and I could just see a hideous bruise forming on his jaw next to his mouth. His bottom lip was split, dried blood caked along the swollen line of the wound.

I dropped to my knees in front of him, my heart pounding so hard I felt like I was going to be sick. "Henry, what happened?" I asked once I found my voice.

He looked up at me, seeming to notice me for the very first time. "Tamara," he said, his voice a ragged croak.

I took the tie from him and put my hand gingerly on his face, running my fingers over his bruise as gently as I could manage. "Who did this?" I whispered, though I knew the answer. There was only one possibility.

He swallowed painfully and shook his head. "I'm fucked, Tam."

"What?"

His face seemed to suddenly break, shattered like the mirror on the wall. He squeezed his eyes shut, his shoulders slumping, and he pitched forward. I caught him in my arms, holding him close against me while he shook. The noise that came out of him was inhuman, like all the months of grief and fear and anger we'd lived through since Isaak disappeared condensed in a single sound. It made my eyes sting, and I struggled to swallow down the burning lump in my throat.

"They've got me," he said. "They've got me and there's nothing I can do. I'm done."

GSAF. But *why*? When were they going to leave us alone?

I didn't ask him anything more. I just ran my fingers through his hair, soft and dark and sleek, and held him against me so tightly I was afraid he might break.

But of course that was impossible. He was already broken. We both were.

CHAPTER 16

- h e n r y -

JANUARY FIRST, 2074. THE SUN WAS TORQUING BLINDING AS I climbed the stairs out of the downtown train station and emerged onto the bustling street. Commuters rushed to and fro, most of them heading for the AresTec campus on Sparta Island with plastic coffee mugs clutched tightly to their chests. Half of them were probably hung over, like me—but, unlike me, they were putting on a good front about it. Last night's festivities forgotten, it was just another workday for them, bright and cloudless and unseasonably cold.

I'd never really pictured myself here, part of the downtown corporate crowd. That seemed like another person's life. But apparently it was going to be mine, now. A new year and a fresh start, in more ways than one. The all-new Henry Sandhu was making his debut today.

They'd finally found a way to make the consequences actually matter to me.

The last time I'd been here, it was totally empty. A stark contrast from today. Clusters of men and women loitered in the lobby, ordering lattes and breakfast muffins from the café next to the elevators. A receptionist sat behind a smooth, U-shaped desk, watching me with narrowed eyes. The bruise on my jaw probably made me look more out of place than I already felt.

I drew my wallet out of the back pocket of my dress slacks. Fortunately, they hadn't gotten torn in the scuffle last night. I'd just needed to iron them this morning to make myself presentable. "Arun Sandhu," I said, handing the woman my I.D. "I have an appointment with Joseph Condor."

"Of course, Mr. Sandhu," she replied, the suspicion fading only slightly from her expression. She opened a side drawer and pulled out a lanyard with a temporary guest I.D. clipped to the end. "I'll let him know you're here. And you'll need to stop by human resources later. They have some new hire forms for you to fill out."

I nodded and took a few steps away from the reception desk, trying to ignore the ringing in my ears as I looked up at the massive metal plaque on the wall over the elevators. The words *Global Space and Astronautics Federation* were blazoned over a crescent emblem, with a Latin motto I'd never bothered to learn the translation of mounted underneath. Isaak could have told me what it meant.

But Isaak was gone. And it was time for me to accept it.

My palmtop buzzed in my pocket, a welcome distraction from the plaque and the Latin and the headache and my stupid, poisonous thoughts. I pulled it out and glanced at it—a text from Tamara.

How r u today? she'd written. *Feeling better?*

I smiled faintly at it, reading the text over and over, hearing her voice saying the words, committing it to memory. Then I pressed delete.

"Mr. Sandhu." I looked up to see Joseph Condor step out of the elevator, moving toward me with a cordial smile on his face. He stopped next to me, ice-blue eyes gleaming. "I'm glad to see you didn't have second thoughts." When I didn't respond, he nodded in satisfaction and clapped me on the shoulder. "Welcome to the team."

"Glad to be here," I said hollowly. "Let's get to work."

AUTUMN

2074 C.E.

Chapter 17

- t a m a r a -

I ALWAYS KNEW THAT IT WAS A LOT HOTTER ON EARTH THAN on Mars, but if July in Arizona was any indication, it was a wonder that people didn't roast alive. Even with the air conditioner running on high in my dressing room, I felt limp and stringy.

The makeup artist blotted my forehead with a triangular sponge and made a tutting sound out of the side of her mouth. "You're melting, my dear," she said.

"I'll probably turn into a puddle right there on the stage," I agreed with a laugh.

She smiled crookedly, brushing a bit more powder across my cheeks and assessing me. "You're going to be fine. And *voila!*" She swiveled my chair around so I could see myself in the mirror. I looked at my reflection appraisingly. It was still a bit of a surreal sight to see myself like this. Today they had me in a purple tank top with white lace along the plunging collar and a short, ruffly black skirt. They'd woven rows of beads into my long brown hair that sparkled when I moved my head from side to side. I looked like a different person. Almost like a star.

Almost.

"Ready to go?" the stage manager called to me from the door.

"As I'll ever be," I said. My stomach was swimming with butterflies, but I'd noticed my anxiety had gotten more manageable with practice. Whenever the panic got too overwhelming, I closed my eyes, took a deep breath and remembered being on that stage at New Year's. The joy of being one with the band, the music, the energy of the crowd. If I had that, I could make it.

One breath at a time. One beat. One note.

"Wait, are you going onstage with that on?" The makeup artist grabbed my hand, running a finger over the yarn bracelet around my left wrist.

"Yes," I said, snatching my hand back. "I am."

She raised her eyebrows. "I don't think Mr. Park is going to like that."

"I don't care. I'm not taking it off."

The tone of my voice said that the matter was closed. She put her hands up and turned away, making a production out of straightening up her makeup kit. I knew that Mr. Park didn't like it. Adam didn't, either. But that was just too bad.

"Five minutes," the stage manager said. He hurried out, followed by the makeup artist. I was alone. Five minutes' peace.

I pulled out my palmtop. It was time for my daily exercise in futility.

Hey, I wrote, my thumb moving quickly across the silky membrane on the palmtop's screen. *I'm in Phoenix now. Arizona. It's super hot. The deserts back home have nothing on this place.*

I sighed, closing my eyes. *The gravity on Earth is awful. Every breath feels like a struggle. Or maybe that's just because I'm nervous. I wish you were here.* I paused, then hit backspace over that last sentence. *I'll be all right, though*, I wrote instead. *I'm used to it by now. Hope you're doing okay. I miss you. Tamara.*

There were so many more words I could write. So much more I wanted to say. *I miss you* never felt like enough. But it was the best I could do.

I hit send, watching the animation of a little paper plane sail across the screen. *Message delivered.* Though I knew it was ridiculous, for just a moment I waited, watching to see if a reply would come in.

But there was nothing. There never was.

"Tamara, we're ready for you."

I nodded, shoving my palmtop into a drawer, and stepped out into the lights.

Chapter 18

- h e n r y -

MONTHS CAN PASS QUICKLY WHEN YOU DON'T GIVE A SHIT anymore. The days seem to blend together, until you're not sure what day or week or year it is, and it doesn't seem to matter anyway.

This was my life now—if it still counted as a life. I'd thought working for the factory was bad, but back then at least I still felt like I had a purpose. Even when I was working, my mind was on a mission. I knew I could go home at the end of the day and get back to my project, get back to trying to find Isaak. There was still a possibility for a future. I'd still had hope. But not now.

Now even my mind was their hostage.

The one thing that got me through was the one thing I wasn't supposed to have. My life revolved around the sound of my palmtop chiming with an incoming text, a few brief sentences to commit to memory before pressing delete and obliterating them from my existence. I felt like a damn junkie waiting for my fix.

I couldn't believe she hadn't stopped yet. And yet I prayed she never would. It was pathetic.

"So, Henry. What do you have for me today?"

I blinked momentarily, trying to remember where I was. Then

reality washed over me, and I pulled off my headset. I was sitting in my office, which for the past several months had been a makeshift coldroom in the basement of the downtown GSAF administrative offices. Not the best environment for this kind of work, but the most convenient—and unobtrusive. Condor was standing just inside the doorway, his arms folded. Time for my daily check-in, to make sure I was still working on what I was supposed to and not running any side projects. As if I hadn't learned my lesson there.

I set my headset down on the floor at my feet, careful not to dislodge the length of cable that ran from the headset to the massive computer bank next to me. On the outside, it looked like a regular—if old-fashioned—mainframe. But the inside was different. Special. I'd never seen anything like this system. And neither had GSAF, or the contractors they'd brought in from AresTec and GalaX, the best in the business. Which was why they needed me. When you have a tough job, you call in the experts.

And if the experts won't take the job, you extort them into it.

"Well, I've figured out that this system works at least partially on physical inputs from the users. Which means it needs to have some way to receive the inputs. There must have been some kind of hardware for that, but I'm assuming we don't have that."

I looked expectantly at Condor for a moment, but his face was an expressionless mask. Right. If they had the hardware for it, it was above my security clearance level.

"So, the next best thing we have is the modern VR headset. That's what this is for." I gestured to the headset at my feet, a sleek visor with a small earpod attached. "I'm working on reprogramming the Speculus operating system to recognize M-

VHLL. From there, I should be able to use it to input commands into the system, and we'll have a better idea of what we're dealing with."

I had a feeling that whatever we were dealing with was also beyond my clearance level. Most things were, which is part of what made this job so incredibly frustrating. I didn't even know what the hardware inside that mainframe looked like. The programming language its operating system used was like nothing I'd ever seen before. It had taken me months to decode what the GalaX contractors working on the project had dubbed *Martian-very high-level programming language*, for lack of a better descriptor. Other programming languages used similar principles of code, like integer-based algorithms. They followed an expected pattern. But this was entirely different. It was like someone who had no knowledge of modern programming theory decided to build a system from scratch.

Or maybe just someone without knowledge of Earth-based theories.

I wasn't supposed to know what I was working on, but it didn't take a supergenius to figure out. The climate-controlled rooms they kept the hardware in, the secrecy surrounding every step? They hid it inside a modern casing, but I suspected that if I took a screwdriver to the mainframe I was working on, I'd find something inside that looked suspiciously similar to the now-missing artifact that Scylla had smuggled off-site. The thing that Isaak disappeared with. Something ancient.

This technology they were trying to access—this was what they were really looking for at Erick's dig site. This was what Emil had found all those years ago. It was the key to everything. And that was the most infuriating thing about this entire situation. I finally had the answers. GSAF had laid them right in my lap. And I couldn't do a damn thing with them.

There were so many days that I thought about looking for Emil, telling him what I'd found. I had no doubt that between the two of us, as insufferable as he was, we could unravel everything, bring the whole thing down.

But I couldn't take the risk. No matter how clever I thought I'd been, GSAF had always been one step ahead of me. They knew my weak spot, knew exactly how to exploit it. I couldn't chance them following through on their threats.

My hands were tied.

"How long do you estimate it will take you to get access?" Condor asked.

I shrugged. "A week, maybe two."

"All right. See to it, then." He started to turn toward the door, but a chime cut through the cold air. In my pocket, my palmtop buzzed. He glanced at me over his shoulder. "Someone's popular." When I didn't move, he added, "What, don't you want to see who it is?"

I wasn't going to let him goad me. Nonchalantly, I slid the palmtop out of my pocket, just catching sight of her name on the lock screen before quickly pressing *delete*, message unread.

He quirked an eyebrow and I shrugged again. "Some girls just don't know how to take a hint," I said.

CHAPTER 19

- t a m a r a -

IT FELT STRANGE TO BE HOME, AFTER THREE MONTHS ON EARTH.
Even after going through the gravity adjustment process, I'd
never felt quite right there; but now that I was home, I felt too
light. I'd stumbled getting off the ship, something that had sent
the paparazzi into a gleeful scramble. I wondered if I would ever
feel normal walking on my own two feet again—or if I'd ever be
able to do so without the whole world staring at me.

So much had changed over the span of just a few months. I
didn't feel any different, but suddenly I was this overnight
celebrity. People on the street stared at me when I walked by,
random strangers came up to me asking for my autograph or a
picture or holo-snap. One of my songs was suddenly the home
music on the Speculus login screen. It was all too much.

And now it was time to pack again, though I'd just barely
managed to *un*pack from the trip to Earth. I'd only been home a
week, but it was move-in weekend at my new dorm starting
tomorrow. That thought made me even more nervous than the
Earth tour had. Between recording, interviews and performances,
I hadn't had a moment's quiet since graduation day. Those three
months of screaming crowds and flashing lights had passed like a

fevered dream. It was like the reality that I was no longer in high school hadn't had a chance to sink in, and now I couldn't bear to face it.

"Do you have enough underwear?" Mom asked, bustling in with a laundry basket stacked high.

"I think so. But it's not like I'm going to be too far away if I need any, right?" I said with a weak laugh. That's what I'd been telling myself all day, every time I felt like crying. I'd been going to Herschel for years—the only difference now was that I was going to live there. Even if I didn't see them every day, my moms were still right there if I needed them.

I wondered if my roommate would like me. I didn't think I would enjoy living with a famous person.

Mom set the laundry basket on my bed, placing a hand on top of the precariously balanced stack of folded clothes for a moment to keep the basket from tipping. Then she came over to where I stood near my desk worrying at the zipper on my suitcase.

"Don't worry, sweetie," she said, placing a warm and reassuring hand on my back.

"I'm not," I replied, but of course she knew that was a lie. She pulled me into a hug, and I let her, resting my head on her shoulder and breathing in the warm, familiar scent of her.

Finally she released me, and I went back to the suitcase. She watched me for a moment, looking over my shoulder at everything I'd stuffed into it so far. "Lot of knick-knacks in there," she teased gently. "Might be hard to lug that thing around."

I chewed on my lip. "Maybe I should take some of it out."

She reached over and pulled out the holo-frame on top, swiping through the pictures I'd stored on it. "This is a good one," she said, turning the frame to show me.

It was a picture of me with Isaak and Henry at our freshman formal. They both looked so tiny in it. I guess I did, too.

I took the frame from her. "I miss this," I said, running my finger across the picture. Henry's 3-D face shimmered beneath my touch.

I could feel Mom watching me as I looked down at the holo. "Have you heard from Henry recently?"

"No." I tried to sound careless about it, but my voice came out sullen.

She nudged my elbow. "He'll come around. You all need time, after everything that's happened."

"I don't want to talk about it."

She nodded, moving back over to my bed and pulling out a handful of clothes. She tucked them neatly into one of my bureau drawers, her hand lingering on the drawer pull. Then she sighed. "Tamara, listen. I know you don't want to talk about it, but Henry—"

"The doorbell!" I interrupted, not because I actually heard anything, but because, really, I did *not* want to talk about it. "I think I heard the doorbell. I'll go check."

Mom surely recognized a diversionary tactic when she saw one, but she didn't stop me. I hurried downstairs, eager to get away from her probing words, when a noise from the front hall caught my attention.

A whisper.

Cautiously, I crept toward the entryway and peered around the corner. There was someone at the door, but I couldn't see who it was—Mama's tall form blocked the doorway.

"He'll let you through, but you have to go quickly," she whispered. "If they catch you before you make it to the arch, you'll never get another chance."

"I'm perfectly aware of that," a man's voice replied, deep and gravelly, a smoker's husky growl. "Don't worry about me. Unlike him and his fool father, I at least have an idea of what to expect on the other side."

I leaned forward, trying to catch a glimpse of who she was talking to. Under the carpet beneath my feet, a floorboard creaked. I jerked back just as Mama started to turn, praying she didn't see me. I stood there, heart pounding, for another moment, but the voices grew too soft for me to hear. Quietly as I could manage, I crept away.

Five minutes later, Mama sauntered into the kitchen, where I was eating Oreos as nonchalantly as I could manage.

"I think we've got a mouse," she declared, reaching into the package and helping herself to a cookie.

I quirked my head at her. "There aren't any mice on Mars."

"Hmm," was all she said in reply. She swallowed the cookie, pulled two more out of the package and strolled back out of the room.

As I stared after her in bewilderment, her voice drifted in from the hall. "Oh, and Tamara? Don't bother checking the security footage. I turned the camera off an hour ago."

I tossed my half-eaten cookie down onto the table in disgust. I swear, my mothers had eyes on the backs of their heads. Maybe it was for the best that I was leaving tomorrow, after all.

CHAPTER 20

- h e n r y -

THE ELEVATOR IN THE GSAF BUILDING WAS LIKE A SPECIALLY-engineered hell.

That wasn't just me being hyperbolic. Elevators in general had never been my favorite place to be, but I was relatively certain that Condor had had a hand in this one specifically to torture me. Because almost every single day when I stepped into that moving metal death-box, the same song came on the radio.

"Oh, God, not this again. What floor you want, buddy?" A man maybe ten years older than me was standing with a woman I recognized from the human resources department, and he looked at me as I stepped onto the elevator, his hand hovering over the control panel.

"Ground floor, thanks," I said.

As the doors swished shut, the woman poked him in the ribs. "What, you don't like T-RT?" she asked, a laugh in her voice.

I cringed internally at that godawful nickname. Some tabloid on Earth had come up with it during her summer tour, since they'd decreed the hot new singing sensation's actual name was too long to be bothered with.

"Ugh, no," the man replied. "Like, I get that she's the first

Martian artist to really get any traction on Earth, but she's just so... *pop*."

The old Henry would have interrupted with a well-thought-out string of vulgarities, possibly followed with a punch to the jaw. But the new Henry was detached. He didn't care what other people said or thought, and especially not about *her*. So I just leaned against the handrail and stared up at the speakers on the ceiling.

"Maybe you're right," the woman said. "Besides, did you hear about that red bracelet thing?"

That caught my attention. I glanced over at them before I could stop myself.

"No, what's that?"

"It's some weird anti-government group that's been popping up around the province. Especially with college students. They all wear red bracelets to show that they're opposed to GSAF or something. T-RT wears one, and she refuses to take it off."

The man made a noise in the back of his throat. "What are they, a bunch of neo-Nazis or something? Some right-wing lunatics?"

"Sorry, hang on," I broke in abruptly. "I forgot something in my office. Can you let me off here?"

The two of them blinked at me while the upbeat refrain of Tamara's new single echoed tinnily around us. "Oh, yeah, sure," the man said, hitting the *stop elevator* button. I nodded at them before disembarking. I may be the new Henry, but I wasn't going to stand there and listen to that any longer. I'd take the stairs the rest of the way.

I stopped outside, trying to catch my breath. On the street, cars zipped past, bright blurs of metal and light. The sun had dipped past the horizon, and AresTec Tower was illuminated, casting neon colors across the river. An animated billboard on the other side of the street played an ad for the new Speculus Nano, *The Ultimate Gaming Experience!* I ran a hand through my hair, letting the cold autumn air nip at my skin and clear my head. My thoughts were a blur, but one thing stood out among the noise: she was still wearing that stupid bracelet of Scylla's, after all this time.

I'd given up fighting. But Tamara hadn't.

"Henry."

I looked up in surprise at the sound of my name. I recognized the voice, the way her tongue curled around the R, but I still couldn't believe my eyes when I saw her standing just two meters away from me.

"Mom... What are you doing here?"

She half-smiled, her expression uncertain. "I wanted to talk to you."

I didn't know how to respond. I stared at her, growing increasingly self-conscious of how I must look, standing here outside the GSAF building in a goddamn suit like some kind of bureaucrat.

"A lot has changed in a year," she said finally. "You've grown. You look... well." I scoffed, and she looked down at her feet. "Your father is retiring soon. He had a back injury, so he can't work as much." She fiddled with her long black braid, pulling it over her shoulder. It was streaked with gray, and it made me realize how much older she looked now. A lot older than she should have. "He's... he is proud of you."

"Oh, of course. He's proud of me now." Now that I was toeing the government line, now that I was working for GSAF as Joseph Condor's unargumentative yes-man. Now that I was just a shell of myself.

My mother took a step closer. "He has always been proud of you. We both have. You are an incredibly talented, intelligent boy. Of course we're proud of you."

I barked out an involuntary laugh. My head was trying to rein me in, remind me that I needed to watch what I said, to remember where I was standing. But when had I ever listened to my head?

"You sure as hell didn't seem proud of me when you threw me out on the street. All those times you told me what a disappointment I was whenever I'd come home late from detention."

"Henry, please." She swallowed. "You have to understand where we're coming from—"

"I've heard it before, Mom."

"No. You haven't." Her voice was so firm that my response died on my tongue. She looked at me with dark, serious eyes. "I have never explained this to you. I didn't want to burden you with it. But maybe that was a mistake."

She sighed, looking across the river at the AresTec building, the LED lights along its façade flashing neon pink, then blue, then green. "When your father and I were your age, the world was being destroyed by war. My father, your Grandpa Henry, he died in combat. I know you knew that. But what we haven't told you is that your father..." She trailed off momentarily, closing her eyes as if not sure whether she should continue. Then she squared her shoulders and looked at me. "Punjab was a very dangerous place in those days, Henry, especially for Sikhs. Your father's family spoke out against corruption. They fought for civil liberties, for equal rights. And... they were killed. Their house was bombed. Only your father and his younger brother survived."

I stared at her, stunned. I struggled to find the right words to say, but none came.

"He went to live with his uncle's family in Delhi, and that is where I met him. He does not like to speak of it, and so we don't. But you need to know the truth if you are to understand why he acts the way he does." She stepped forward, brushing my hair away from my face like she used to when I was a kid. "Henry, your father and I came here because we wanted to raise our child in a world without war. It's hard to see the beauty in life when there's so much death around you. We didn't want that for you. The whole purpose of GSAF was to ensure that this world doesn't suffer the way our home world did. GSAF promised to bring us a world without war. The last thing I wanted was for my child—my precious son—to get caught up in the kinds of troubles that killed our families and friends on Earth. And then you did anyway."

I swallowed down the lump in my throat. "Mom," I said, my voice ragged, "I'm sorry. I didn't—"

"I know you didn't know, Henry. It's not your fault. When your father kicked you out of the house, it was just because he didn't know how to explain. He thought if he took away your comfort, you'd finally bend. That you would see reason. But I should have known that wouldn't work." She chuckled. "You're too stubborn."

But I did bend, I thought in disgust. *It just took a different kind of threat to do the trick.* I suddenly felt furious with myself, knowing that my dad's family had died standing up for their principles, but I'd been so quick to throw mine to the wind.

My mother put her hand on my shoulder, drawing my attention back to her. "I've realized over this year... I can't change you, Henry. I just want the best for you, but you're an adult now. You have to do what you have to do. And even if I don't agree with you, I'm just happy to have you at all. You don't have to do this. You don't have to work for GSAF if you don't want to. I will love you no matter what."

The lump in my throat was back. Mom reached her arms out and I leaned down into her embrace. "Thank you, Mom," I said quietly.

She pulled away, looking up at me. "Thank Tamara."

I looked at her in confusion. "Tamara?"

Mom nodded. "She's the reason I finally got the courage to come here. She called me this morning and told me she didn't want you to be alone on this day."

"This day?" I repeated, and then I realized with a jolt what day it was. The last day of October.

Isaak's birthday. I'd forgotten. But Tamara remembered.

I inhaled deeply, turning thoughtfully to look up at the GSAF building behind me. "Yeah. She was right." I took my mom's hand. "And I'm glad you came. This is an important day."

I wouldn't forget again.

Chapter 21

♫

- t a m a r a -

I WOKE UP WITH MY FACE PRESSED INTO THE HARD SURFACE OF my desk. I groggily lifted my head, looking around to get my bearings. I was in my dorm room, my Casio askew on my desktop. I guess I'd fallen asleep doing my homework. I'd been exhausted after I got back to Herschel Island from my private vigil down at the cove. Crying that much never helped.

"Have a nice nap?" my roommate Mariyah asked, the hint of a chuckle in her voice. I turned to see her sitting at her own desk, her sketch pencils scattered all around her and a smudge of charcoal across her cheeks. She was a studio art major, so this was pretty much her signature Look. She hadn't been here earlier; she must have come in after I fell asleep.

"Not really," I admitted. My left shoulder felt pinched from the angle I'd been sleeping at, and I still had that disoriented feeling that came along with a particularly vivid dream. This one had been really bizarre, and I had gotten used to having weird dreams over the last annum. I'd dreamed that I was sick: some kind of mysterious disease that was eating me from the inside out, leaving few visible marks but killing me thoroughly nonetheless. The physical repercussions of a secret. Just a dream, but all too real.

The doctors had asked if there was anyone they should call for me, and there was only one person I wanted to see. I knew he had the disease, too. He was part of the secret, and it was eating him alive as well. But he was stronger than me. He might pull through. At least he'd make it longer than me.

In the dream, he'd held me tight as uneven dark splotches spread under my skin, devoured me alive. But I'd felt weirdly calm, even though I hurt—the real-life aches from how I was hunched breaking through my sleep, I think—because he was there.

It should have been a nightmare, considering that I'd been dying. Still, irrationally, I almost wanted to go back to sleep so he'd at least still be there.

It was pathetic, considering that I hadn't seen him face-to-face in ten months. But I couldn't turn it off. It was just how I felt. I'd been having dreams like this for months, my subconscious betraying me. I missed him so much. Losing Isaak had been bad enough, but Henry pushing me away was almost worse. Because he hadn't disappeared into thin air. He'd just made it clear that he didn't want me around anymore.

Too bad I couldn't seem to stop wanting him.

Mariyah watched me as I rubbed crust out of my eyes and fiddled with the audio editor on my deskpad, checking to make sure it had saved the file I'd been working on before I dozed off. Something about it seemed wrong, off-beat and out of sync. I couldn't figure out what was wrong with it. Maybe it was just me.

"You were talking in your sleep again," Mariyah said, a smirk playing at her lips.

My hand hovered over the Casio motionlessly. That was an embarrassing fact about myself I hadn't known until I had a roommate: I was a sleep talker. At least Mariyah had been nice about it. But that seemed to be par for the course with her. So far she'd basically been the dream roommate, friendly and low-key, like someone I'd known forever. And best of all, she treated me like I was normal—something I never realized I would miss until it was too late. I wasn't T-RT to her. I was just Tamara.

Casually, I said, "Yeah?"

"You said something that started with an H." Her smirk deepened. She was teasing me, though I knew she didn't mean it maliciously. Between hanging out with me and Scylla every weekend and my unconscious midnight babble, she'd heard a lot of that name.

My face undoubtedly as red as Mariyah's hijab, I shrugged. "I don't remember what I was dreaming about," I lied.

I could feel her eyes on me a moment longer, but I tried to ignore her stare. Then she said, "Your palmtop went off a minute ago."

"Oh?" I tapped on the screen, expecting something from my moms or from Adam or maybe from one of my classmates. I'd stopped hoping for anything else months ago. But my heart stopped when I saw it was a message from Henry.

Thank you.

I read it over and over, not sure I was seeing it right. But it didn't disappear when I closed my eyes. It was real.

"Hmm, what's that face?" Mariyah said, unsuccessfully trying to hide the glee in her voice. I glanced over at her, blinking away the stinging sensation behind my eyes. She couldn't have known who had texted me, but obviously my expression said it all.

"It's nothing," I replied, though I couldn't quite manage to wipe the smile off my face.

"If you say so," she sang, and now I did laugh. I slipped my headphones back on, and this time, when I pressed *play* on my audio file, the music sounded sweet to my ears.

WINTER

2074 C.E.

Chapter 22

- h e n r y -

I PULLED MY JACKET MORE TIGHTLY AROUND MYSELF AND breathed out, watching a cloud of fog fan out from my mouth and dissipate. Sourly, I wondered why they were still bothering with the air conditioner in here when it was close to freezing outside. Winter had Mars firmly in its clutches, and this was one of the coldest years I'd lived through. But despite the cold temperatures, it hadn't snowed. It hadn't even rained in months. We were all on mandatory water conservation rations now, with hefty fines for those who used more than their allotment. Nobody wanted to use the word "drought," but you could feel it hovering like a silent cloud over everyone's minds.

Everything went straight to hell when Isaak disappeared.

A soft chime cut through the cold, quiet air. Not my palmtop—this was more muted. A Speculus notification. I pulled the visor over my face, adjusting the earpiece and activating it. The notification bubble appeared in the open air before my eyes. *Operation successful.*

I was in. This was the point at which I was supposed to call for Joseph Condor to bring in someone with a higher security level. My role at this stage would be done. They'd dismiss me, and when I came back tomorrow, there'd be something new for me to work on. I'd never know what it was, exactly, I'd been trying to break into for all these months.

But I was done playing by their rules.

A command window hovered in the empty space before me, awaiting my input. This was my last chance to turn back.

Instead, I entered the system.

I was bombarded with more of the strange symbols that had been plaguing me throughout this whole project, the unfamiliar alphanumeric system that made M-VHLL so damn incomprehensible. It was like I had jumped into a rushing river of foreign information. Images I didn't recognize, glyphs I couldn't read, words I didn't understand. I squeezed my eyes shut in frustration, but a rush of sound still assaulted my ears.

"God, I don't want any of this," I muttered in frustration. "I just want the answers."

As if in response to my words, the cacophony fell silent. I opened my eyes.

And there he was.

It was a vid file of some kind. It must have been filmed with a VR camera, the kind that record from the wearer's perspective, because it moved and turned like a first-person video game that I couldn't control. A man's voice spoke in my ear, muffled, in a language I didn't understand. And then he turned his head, and there was Isaak.

He was wearing strange clothing, like a uniform, silvery blue and skintight. His face was dirty, red grime clinging to his hairline. Around the top of his cranium was some kind of metallic probe thing. It looked straight out of a science fiction flick.

"Who are you people?" he asked. "Where am I? Are you with GSAF?"

GSAF. I knew it. They had him, they'd had him all along. What the hell were they doing to him, though? Some kind of experiment? What was it doing on this computer, then?

The man with the camera said something back to him in a soft, soothing voice, and walked closer to Isaak, who watched him warily. He reached out, placing a dark hand on Isaak's shoulder, and then said something else and gestured to the probe on Isaak's brow.

"What is this thing?" Isaak demanded, his voice sounding panicked. "Are you doing something to my brain?"

I sucked in my breath involuntarily and cursed. At the sound of my voice, the vid flickered and Isaak disappeared from my screen. "Wait, no!" I protested out loud. "Bring Isaak back!"

The program obeyed, but the original video didn't return. It flickered, and now there was a girl in the room, a Black girl with bleached white hair pulled up in a braid, an earpod of some kind hanging out of her right ear. Isaak was sitting on the foot of a hospital bed scowling at her.

"What is the System, anyway?" he asked. I noticed that the probe was off his head now, but he also wore an earpod. "You people go on about it every other word. The most I can figure is that it's some kind of mind-reader. Which is not creepy at all."

I blinked as she responded to him in the unfamiliar language. *The System? Mind-reader?* Did he mean this? The technology GSAF had me working on—it could read your thoughts?

It hadn't responded to my thoughts so far, but it had responded to my words. Maybe it was because I wasn't using the proper hardware with it. Speculus wasn't designed to read your brain, as far as I knew. But it did have a microphone.

I had to test it. "Show me more," I said.

And it did.

I don't know how much time had passed when I heard the door behind me open. It didn't register, at first; I was too engrossed in my find. I couldn't tear my attention away. But then I felt the hand on my shoulder.

"Sandhu, what are you doing?"

Yesterday, that voice, the knowledge that I was caught—it would have made my blood run cold. But now it made it boil. I didn't know how long I had been in here, whether it was just a few minutes or a few hours. But in that time, everything changed.

I pulled the Speculus headset off my face and stared at Joseph Condor. His blue eyes met my black ones, and for the first time since I'd known him, he almost looked afraid.

"I think the question is," I said, "what are *you* doing?"

CHAPTER 21

- t a m a r a -

THE DOOR OPENED, AND I LOOKED UP. MY HEART WAS ALREADY beating in my throat before I even saw him, but when that metal door opened and he came through, an officer holding his arm, it just stopped.

When he saw me, he halted midstep. We stared at each other for a long minute. I had so much I wanted to say to him, but now that he was here in front of me, no words would come.

"Tamara," Henry said finally, his voice rough at the edges. "What are you doing here?"

I smiled hesitantly. "Scylla called me." She'd called to tell me that Henry had gotten arrested, but that hadn't been all she'd said. Everything they'd been keeping from me for the last year— suddenly it all made sense.

But I still wasn't sure I could believe it.

He made a face. "Scylla was supposed to come bail me out." He seemed annoyed, which made me annoyed. So much for a happy reunion.

"Scylla couldn't afford bail," I said, glaring back at him.

He didn't respond. The two of us looked down uncomfortably, avoiding each other's gazes.

I watched silently as Henry scrawled his signature on the digital reader and the clerk handed him back his palmtop and wallet. Neither of us spoke again until we were on the front steps of the station. I stopped just outside the doors, pulling up the hood of my jacket and wrapping my scarf so it partially obscured my face.

"Seriously?" Henry said, looking at me crookedly, his eyebrow quirked.

"If someone recognizes me here, I'll be in even more trouble with my manager than I already have been for this bracelet thing."

"Oh." His expression changed, softened imperceptibly. "Tamara," he said, barely audible. I moved a step closer, to hear him better. "Thank you. You didn't have to come here tonight. I know I've..." He swallowed. "I've been a dick to you this annum. And I had a reason, I promise. It wasn't... it wasn't because I wanted to."

My heart stumbled, hope swelling in me as I remembered what Scylla had said when she called me. The things I didn't— couldn't—believe. I waited for his next words, but they didn't come. He looked down, his features obscured by the thick curtain of his black hair. He was retreating into himself again.

Trying to suppress my disappointment, I hooked my hand around his arm. "Come on," I said. "I'll walk you home."

We walked in silence for a few moments, my heart beating irregularly as I held onto his elbow. I kept expecting him to push me away, but he didn't. So, at last, I said softly, "Do you want to tell me what happened?"

I already knew what he was going to say. "*It's nothing.*" He wouldn't tell me anything, and then he'd disappear again. I was stupid to think tonight would be any different than the last year had been.

"GSAF has Isaak," Henry said.

I stopped dead in my tracks, almost losing my grip on his arm. But then he stopped too, reaching out to steady me.

"What?" I whispered.

He nodded. "And I have proof."

And then he told me. Everything.

GSAF had blackmailed him into working for them after New Year's. That much I'd known already—he'd told Scylla some things, and she told me the rest. But hearing the words from Henry's mouth made it more real, somehow. All these months, he'd been in the belly of the beast. And now he had proof. GSAF had Isaak. They'd had him all along.

"When I saw him on those vids, I just... lost it," Henry said. "I couldn't do it anymore. Condor came in, and we got into it, and the next thing I knew..." He shrugged. "They called the cops."

I swallowed. "You're sure it was him?"

He nodded. "I couldn't understand everything he was saying. In a lot of them he was speaking some language I didn't recognize. But it was him. I don't know where they're keeping him, but they have him. They've got to."

"How old do you think the vids are?" I asked.

He frowned. "I'm not sure. But they can't be that old. GSAF has only had the ability to decode M-VHLL for a few months. If this System has a record of him, then it must have been taken sometime after they got it back online. He might..." He hesitated, his voice cracking. "He might still be alive."

I held onto Henry's arm for support while the ground beneath me swayed. "Tamara..." He turned, putting his hands on my shoulders in a steadying grip. "Tamara, listen. I know this is a shock. It will be okay, I promise you. We'll find him. I know how you must be feeling right now."

I don't think he did.

My hood had slipped, and he pulled it back up to shield my face, his palm brushing across my cheek as he did so. That simple touch was enough to send my world reeling again. He started to move his hand away, but I reached up and caught it with my fingers. My heart pounded as Scylla's words from earlier echoed in my mind.

"I'm tired of covering this up. Do you want to know why he's been avoiding you since New Year's? The real reason GSAF finally got him over to their side?"

"Henry," I said. His face was so close I felt drunk with it. All these months of being without him had turned me into a lightweight. "Scylla said something else earlier. I need to know if it was true."

His expression turned wary. "What did Scylla tell you?"

Part of me didn't want to say it. If Scylla was wrong, I would ruin everything.

But I needed to know the truth. I couldn't keep on like this anymore. This year had been torture. I couldn't go through that again. So I summoned my courage.

"She said that the reason you stopped talking to me for all those months was to protect me. That on New Year's, GSAF threatened—me." I stumbled over that word, realizing how arrogant it must sound. It was ridiculous. I shouldn't have said anything.

Henry exhaled and looked away from me. "That's true."

I stared at him, the meaning his words washing over me. "But, Henry, why didn't you tell me? We could have fought them."

"I wasn't going to take that risk."

"But why?"

He shook his head, still not looking at me. "Do you really have to ask that?"

And there were Scylla's words ringing in my ears again: "*Because he loves you, Tamara. Because to Henry, you're the only thing that matters. He'd do anything to protect you, even if it killed him.*"

He loved me.

He started to pull away. "Look, it doesn't matter. It's not important."

"Yes, it is."

I barely heard myself speak the words, but I saw the way they hit Henry. He turned, meeting my eyes with surprising vulnerability. "What?"

"It's important. *You're* important." I stepped forward, hesitantly reaching out, my fingers brushing his chest. "I don't want you to keep things from me. I don't want you to suffer like this anymore. I can't bear it. Because to me"—I shivered as he covered my hand with his—"to me, you're the only thing that matters."

I can't say whose lips met whose first; whether he bent his head down to mine or I dragged it there. All I know is that it wiped every thought out of my mind entirely. This was nothing like my first kiss had been, full of embarrassment and regrets. His touch turned me to fire, lit my skin with flame and starlight. I wanted it to consume me, wanted nothing but to burn, as long as he was with me.

At long last, everything was right. And my heart was singing.

CHAPTER 24

- h e n r y -

EVERYTHING CHANGES.

I thought everything changed when Isaak disappeared, but maybe that was my first mistake. Because everything that had happened, everything that had changed—GSAF, Tierra Nueva, all of Mars—even me—those changes had started long before. I just hadn't noticed until it was too late. I'd been reactive to everything. I'd let the events around me guide my path, rather than charting it myself. That's how GSAF always managed to stay one step ahead of me. Because I didn't want to alter my course. No matter what I'd said, deep down, I'd wanted everything to stay the same. To go back to normal.

But life's not like that. Things change, whether you want them to or not. And you have to be ready for them. You have to be willing to change yourself.

It was time for me to start being proactive.

Chapter 25

- t a m a r a -

I MANAGED TO STAY ON MY LITTLE CLOUD OF JOY FOR A FEW hours afterward, refusing to let the thoughts back in. I pulled out my deskpad, opened my composition app, and wrote some music for a while, the notes flowing from my heart onto the screen, a white wall covered in lovely black lines and dots.

I was still floating when Mariyah came home from the studio, her cheeks smudged with paint this time instead of charcoal. "Well," she said, looking me over appraisingly, "someone's happy."

I grinned. "Yup."

She turned her desk chair around, sitting side-saddle on it and leaning her elbows against the chair back. "So? Aren't you going to tell me what happened?"

My cheeks felt delightfully warm as I shoved my deskpad aside and spilled. Well, not the parts about GSAF. Mariyah knew that the boy who had disappeared from Tierra Nueva last annum had been my friend, but I hadn't filled her in on any of the stuff about the dig site or the government's involvement. The rest of it was hard enough to believe on its own, and the last thing I needed was to land Mariyah on GSAF's watch list, too.

But I told her that I had seen Henry, finally. And that one

thing had led to another.

"Well, well, Miss Tamara," Mariyah laughed when I was through. "That was refreshingly bold of you."

My face grew hotter. "Do you think it was wrong of me?"

She scoffed. "What, that you kissed Henry?"

"Yeah. I mean, with everything that happened with Isaak..." And was still happening, though I didn't tell Mariyah that. The guilt was nagging at the back of my mind. Isaak was locked in some government bunker there, and I'd just made out with his best friend. "I feel like I'm being selfish."

"Why?"

"I mean... Isaak liked me."

Mariyah made a face. "So, what, only one person in the world is ever allowed to like you? And if that one person happens to vanish off the face of the planet, you're off the shelf for life?" When I avoided her eyes, she stood, pushing in her desk chair and coming to crouch in front of me. "Tamara, listen. This isn't some dumb chick flick where you're caught in a love triangle, this is real life. You're allowed to have feelings. And your feelings can change. That's perfectly normal. A lot of time has passed. Things aren't going to be the same forever, that's just life. So you shouldn't feel guilty about it."

I smiled and nodded, and she stood, ruffling my hair. "Honestly, I'm just glad you guys finally worked this out. Scylla and I were both getting sick of your mutual pining sessions. If you didn't get your acts together soon, we were planning to run an intervention."

I gawked at her. "You talked about this with Scylla?" I didn't dare mention that Scylla actually had run an intervention, she'd never let me live it down.

"Duh." She sat back down at her desk. "That's what friends do. Gossip about their other friends. Just make sure you invite us both to the wedding. I think we deserve it, after all you've put us through."

"Yeah," I said, drumming my fingers on my desk. I needed to text Scylla and thank her.

"But first," Mariyah went on, "I think it's high time I meet this Henry person. I need to make sure he's worthy of dating my roommate."

I laughed. "That will be an encounter for the ages." I turned back to my deskpad, humming to myself. Mariyah grinned, tapping her pencil in time. Before long we were singing together, belligerently, unapologetically off-key, and laughing until we cried.

Isaak was alive. We'd find him. And Henry loved me. That was all that mattered. Everything was going to be okay.

It was the best night I'd had in ages.

The next morning, I'd come down a bit. A night's sleep had put distance between me and the events of the evening, and it was all starting to feel surreal. Especially since I hadn't heard anything from Henry since I'd left him at the dock after he walked me back to the ferry. What if he'd gotten cold feet?

By the time I got out of class that afternoon, I was starting to worry that last night had been a dream—that he was going to go right back to cutting me out of his life. The thought made me feel bereft.

"You're being ridiculous," I said to myself. "Just text him." I pulled out my palmtop, tapping something out, changing my mind and backspacing over it. I finally settled on a casual, *How r u today?*

I stared down at my palmtop after pressing send, my heart racing, certain he wasn't going to answer.

But then he did.

I almost did a giddy happy dance on the spot. *Good*, he'd written. *R u out of class?* When I said that I was, he texted back, *Can u meet me on the boardwalk at 4? I have an idea.*

I smirked. *That sounds ominous*, I wrote, but of course I would be there. Nothing could have kept me away.

At quarter to four, I was already waiting in front of Napoleon's, looking out over the railing at the rolling waves in the bay. The sound of footsteps behind me made me turn, but I didn't recognize the man approaching me from across the boardwalk.

Or, at least, I thought I didn't. Then he tapped me on my shoulder and I did a double-take. A bit taller than me, dark and muscular, wearing one of his familiar old t-shirts despite the freezing cold. But his hair was gone. I realized with a start that he'd cut it all off.

"Henry," I said, staring at him in shock. "What did you do?"

He ducked his head, a familiar gesture, but this time there was no black curtain to hide his face behind. For once, I could see the slight blush forming on his cheeks. "I cut it. Do you like it?"

I reached up, pulling at the short wisps curling over his forehead. "What are you trying to do, disguise yourself so you can go into hiding?"

He laughed, catching my fingers and holding them. "No. I'm not running anymore. I just decided that it's time for me to be serious."

"You can't be serious with long hair?" I asked, but it was mostly rhetorical. I knew it was selfish—it shouldn't matter to me how he wore his hair, it was none of my business—but he looked ridiculously attractive with his hair cut this way. Maybe it was because I could actually see his face now.

He smirked. "Well, other people don't think so. And I need them to take me seriously if we're going to succeed."

"You've thought this through."

"I have. Do you have a minute? I'll tell you all about it." He laced his fingers through mine, and I looked down at them, my own face flushing now.

"Yeah," I said. "And I'll tell you what I've been up to today, too."

He led me down to the beach, to the rocky outcropping that jutted out into the bay. He climbed up onto a boulder looking over the water, pulling me up next to him. Then he drew a memory card out of his pocket. "This is it," he said.

"What?"

"Everything. Everything that I managed to get out of GSAF about the System before Condor caught me. The proof is all right here."

I took the card, turning it over and back between my fingers. "And what are you going to do with it?"

"I'm blowing the whistle. I need to do it quickly, before they can shut me up."

Before they made him disappear, he meant. I wouldn't let that happen. I already had a plan in motion.

"I talked to Wyatt," I said. "He's going to work on getting his mom on our side."

Henry looked at me in surprise. "What?"

I nodded. GSAF had caught us all off-guard when they took Isaak. That wouldn't happen again. "He said he's tired of this cover-up. He wants to know what happened to Isaak as much as the rest of us. So if he can help, he will."

Henry looked at me with wide eyes. For a minute I thought he was going to argue with me. But then he smiled and took my hands between his. "Thank you. I'll have to call Ponsford later and thank him, too. Now, here's what I'm thinking…"

He kept his hand on my wrist as he spoke, absently running his thumb over the red bracelet. He had more energy than I'd seen from him in almost two annums. His plan was dangerous, but I wasn't going to argue with him about it anymore. He was right. If we were ever going to help Isaak, we couldn't keep running away, letting GSAF call the shots.

We had to fight.

We talked it all out, until the sun started to dip behind the horizon and the wind picked up, bitterly cold, and he pulled me close and we didn't speak anymore. Everything was changing. I could feel it. But this time, I knew that it was going to be okay.

SPRING

2075 C.E.

.

CHAPTER 26

- h e n r y -

FROM THEN ON, NOTHING WAS THE SAME. BUT THIS TIME I WAS
ready for whatever the future held.

Tierra Nueva was the first thing that changed. Once the
media picked up on my leak, the fire spread too quickly for GSAF
to put it out. I went public with everything—that Isaak's
disappearance had been linked to the secret technology buried
out in the hills. That the early habitability analysis had proved
there was life here before, and they covered it up. That GSAF was
trying to secretly access this technology in order to spy on our
minds. I told them everything, and this time I had proof.

The people of Mars weren't exactly happy to learn that the
governments of Earth had been lying about the existence of pre-
colonial life. But they really didn't like that *spying-on-our-brains*
thing. There were protests in the street, and I'm not talking the
kind that Scylla organized. These ran a little closer to *riots*. There
were no glitter-bombed posterboards to be found at these rallies,
just angry citizens that GSAF had finally pushed too far.

I saw ProLibertate at a couple of them. To say he was pleased
with this turn of events would be an understatement. "You
started all this, man," he said, clapping me firmly on the back.

"You lit the fire."

Yeah, I lit the fire. And I was the first one it burned. Joseph Condor was out for my blood, with a vengeance. But Governor Ponsford had granted me temporary amnesty pending an investigation. For the time being, GSAF couldn't touch me—and that included Condor. I couldn't leave Tierra Nueva, but that was fine. I wasn't planning on going anywhere. This was my home, and I was going to fight for it. I was going to fight for our liberty.

I could see the cracks forming between Wyatt's mom and her lieutenant governor. The provincial government—hell, the government of all of Mars—was being pulled in two different directions, those faithful to Earth and those who thought the time was right for us to sever our ties. Only time would tell which side would win out.

But I had hope. Public opinion was changing. GSAF's approval ratings were at an all-time low. GalaX was under scrutiny, scrambling to distance themselves from their government connections. For the first time, it felt like maybe there was hope. That an independent Mars wasn't a pipe dream.

But we'd have to fight for it. Because Earth wasn't ready to give us up that easily. GSAF clamped down on the protests almost immediately. The police were quickly militarized—you couldn't walk down the street without a tank driving past.

Mars had become a warzone, and Tierra Nueva was the front lines.

The last week of May-II, Scylla organized one more rally. A special one. Tamara talked to Wyatt and got us clearance: access to the place where all of this started, the place none of us had set foot for two annums, a full Martian year.

The dig site.

Everyone made the journey out from Tierra Nueva and Curiosity Bay. Well, almost everyone. Isaak's mom still wanted nothing to do with us, and her new husband Erick Gomez went along with her decision. And, of course, we were missing Emil.

The world had been eager to find him after the news broke about GSAF's cover-up. His old apartment building was crawling with investigative reporters eager to be the first to get an interview with the disgraced scientist who'd been proved right after all these years. But Emil was nowhere to be found. No one had seen him in months. No one knew where he'd disappeared to.

I got a sour taste in my mouth whenever I thought about it. Because I couldn't shake the feeling that Emil and Isaak had wound up in the same place.

The sun shone down brightly on the crater that afternoon. It was spring again, and being here, it almost felt like no time had passed at all. Like we'd just come out here to dig, to keep searching for answers, for Isaak's underground kingdom of the Little Green Men. And yet it also felt like a lifetime. Back then, the most security there'd been on the site were a few drone cameras. Now there were officers in riot gear lining the perimeter of the gathering area, and suited GSAF agents carrying assault rifles dotting the craters. The difference was palpable. It made me miss the old days, when everything had been easier.

Onward and upward.

Tamara had some of her contacts set a stage up for us in the large, flat area we'd once used as a parking lot. I stood there now, looking out over the crowd that had assembled in front of us. Most of them were strangers, but some I recognized—the

Triple-C guys, Wyatt and his girlfriend, Tamara's roommate Mariyah. There were a surprising number of faces I remembered from the Academy, people that, back then, used to make fun of us in the hallway. It was hard not to begrudge them showing their faces here, acting like Isaak had ever been a friend of theirs. But then I remembered that, regardless of how I felt, the fact that they were here meant that they weren't afraid to take a stand against GSAF. And right now, that was the most important thing.

Tamara hurried up the steps onto the stage where Scylla and I were already waiting. The three of us, the ones who'd gotten caught up in this mess along with Isaak, were each going to give a speech. "The sound system's set up," Tamara said, running her hand over the lapel of my jacket to smooth it. Six months later, I still hadn't gotten quite used to the way my heart flip-flopped whenever she touched me. I wasn't sure I ever would. "Are you guys ready?"

"No," Scylla said. I glanced over at her sallow face. She looked like she was going to throw up. "But you might as well start. I'll manage."

"You go after Henry," Tamara said, squeezing her hand reassuringly. "I'll go last."

"That way if you puke on the audience, it won't stick out in their minds as much," I added. Scylla punched my arm, but I noticed that some of the color went back into her cheeks.

I started to turn toward the podium, but then I hesitated. This all felt so surreal, like I was walking through a dream.

"Hey." Tamara put her hand on my cheek, giving me the lightest of kisses that still managed to burn straight through to my core. "You'll be fine."

I nodded, checked the red bracelet on my wrist to make sure it was still there—and walked to the podium.

I looked out over the crowd for a minute, watching as they all quieted down, turned to face me. Several of them were holding signs, posters that read *Where's Isaak?* or *End the GSAF Cover-Up.*

"Hey, everyone," I said, running an awkward hand through my short-cropped hair. "Thank you for coming today. As most of you know, this marks the one year—one Martian year, that is—anniversary of the disappearance of Isaak Contreras." My voice echoed strangely across the hillside, and I paused, trying to adjust to the sound.

"I heard some people earlier call this a memorial, but it's not. Because a memorial is what you have when someone's died. And I truly believe, in my heart of hearts, that Isaak is not dead."

A noise in the distance broke through my words. A few murmurs rose up from the crowd, people glancing over their shoulders to see what the commotion was. I frowned and swallowed before continuing.

"Over the last several months, the Free Mars movement has done incredible work to try to increase government transparency, but we still don't have answers. We still don't know where Isaak is. But I'm not giving up. I refuse to stop until I know. I won't stop until Isaak is released and is back home, safe and sound."

I cleared my throat, looking out over the crowd. "Isaak was..."

As I spoke, my gaze fell on someone standing at the back of the crowd. A tall, lanky teenager with curly brown hair, wearing an odd looking silver body suit. Next to him stood an older man in a filthy factory uniform, and a girl with a curly mane of bleached-white hair. And if I'd had any doubt about who these people were, the man leading them into the clearing clinched it: Joseph Condor.

I broke off midsentence, staring in disbelief. It seemed impossible, but though his clothes were unfamiliar, I knew that face.

It couldn't be. It just couldn't. But it was.

It was Isaak.

The adventure continues in *New World*,
Book Two of the Iamos Trilogy,
available now from Snowy Wings Publishing.

Want more now? Turn the page for
a special bonus short story set in
the world of Iamos.

WHAT MAKES SOMETHING WORTH LIVING FOR? WHAT MAKES something worth dying for?

On Iamos, the fourth world, the answer was simple. It was the only solution left, really, to a dwindling people on a dying planet. The answer was what the *geroi* had given us, and there was no questioning it.

We live for each other.

It was a phrase uttered reassuringly, a balm for souls worn raw by the devastating realization that our atmosphere was draining away, that we had somehow gone too far and pushed the planet too hard and now there was nothing left for us. It was the key to our survival. It was the end of chaos, panic, uncertainty. We no longer had to wonder or live in fear of the unknown. The *geroi* had given us the Progression, and they had given us the solution. They pledged to us that all lives were one. If we followed them, our species would survive. We had to, because we lived for each other.

There was another side to it, of course. The implicit other half that few conceived of and none dared speak aloud. That was, of course:

We die for each other.

This was something that I hadn't considered much growing up. All my life, I knew only one thing: I existed for the good of the collective. The certainty that our lives were bound to one another meant that we each had a duty, a contract to fulfill. I knew my responsibility was to contribute to the welfare of Iamos, and if I upheld my end of the bargain, I was guaranteed security and relative comfort. That was all that mattered to me, then.

I was born several years after the Progression, when the old government had been replaced by the *geroi* and the castes; but I was lucky enough to have been born a *patroin*, a member of the elite class. I never knew my parents. With the Progression had come the eugenicists, dictating who was allowed to reproduce and when. As with all the other children on Iamos, I was raised by the collective, not by an individual family.

From an early age, I was earmarked to be an Enforcer. Although it was a position of honor and prestige, the truth of the matter was that Enforcers basically did the *geroi's* grunt work. The *gerotus* made the laws, and we made sure they were followed. We were the tax collectors, the police, the soldiers, all in one. We kept the *plivoi* in their places, and we kept the *geroi's* hands clean.

When I reached adolescence, I was apprenticed to an officer who taught me everything there was to know about the job I'd been assigned. Even as a *patroin*, my education was limited. I knew how to read and write, how to use an earpiece and interact with a System panel. This, I suppose, set me apart from the *plivoi*, who were lucky if they could read a few sentences at most. But in retrospect, I realize my education was entirely structured to make me a useful tool for the *geroi*. History, philosophy, the subjects that encouraged critical thinking—those were reserved for the ruling class, the handful of *geroi* who control the destiny of everyone on Iamos. But at the time, none of that mattered to me. I was a *patroin*, and so I was above. Enforcing the will of the *geroi* was more than just my duty, it was an honor. It was a calling I was blessed to have been born into. I believed that.

Then.

It was just a few months before my *enilikin* when Ketros—the Enforcer I was assigned to—and I were sent out to a farm in the valley near the inland sea. Construction on Bright Horizon had been completed the year before I started my apprenticeship, but life was still livable Outside, barely. The *patroi* had settled into the safety of their subterranean villas, where the thick rock walls provided an extra layer of protection against the deadly solar radiation of the world above; and, after a long process of applications and screening, the eugenicists had finalized their admittance list, hand-picking the *plivoi* drudges who would be given the gift of life in exchange for service to the *geroi*. Their less worthy, less *useful* peers, on the other hand, had a choice: peaceful euthanasia, or the slow death of exposure and suffocation Outside.

And I got to be the one to deliver the verdict of life and death to the *plivoi*. Me and Ketros.

The once-fertile valley the farm was nestled in had become all but a desert by the day Ketros and I rode our *gurzas* down the slopes of the surrounding hills. The air that whistled through my nostrils was dry and bitterly cold. I could see a narrow strip of green bisected by a tiny trickle of a stream that was all but gone, leeched away by the vicious winds that sapped more of our atmosphere every day. Parched, dead shoots, remnants of failed crops, checkered the rusty patchwork of ground.

At the foot of the hill, I touched a finger to my earpiece,

pulling up a System panel outlining all the details about this case. The System was the very heart of Iamos. It was more than a computer—had become much greater than that centuries ago. It was linked into our nervous systems, responding to our thoughts, manipulating our hearing and our vision. It knew the thoughts of every living being on Iamos, networking our brains inside and out. It connected everyone on the planet, ensuring that the edicts were fulfilled and alerting the Enforcers of any deviation.

We were nearly upon the farmhouse when a middle-aged woman hurried out to greet us. She seemed nervous, rubbing her hands on the fabric of her clothing. "*Kyrios, Kyrin*," she said with a shaky voice. "You honor us with your presence. My partner and our apprentice are out in the field right now, but they'll have seen your *gurzas* and should be here shortly."

"Very well," Ketros replied, sounding bored. "We'll wait for them inside." He didn't wait for her to invite us in. A *patros* needed no invitation from a *plivoin*. As I followed him inside, I thought I noticed a shadow of movement behind the dirty glass of one of the windows of the house. I watched it with narrowed eyes momentarily, then continued through the door into the front room of the small abode.

We remained in silence for a few minutes, Ketros seated in a dingy armchair with an expression of marked disinterest on his face; myself perched on the edge of a creaking woven fiber stool; and the *plivoin* shifting anxiously from one foot to the other as she stood deferentially in the doorway. Before long, we heard the clamor of footsteps hurrying up the front walkway, and the door flew open. An older man—surely the woman's partner—hurried in, a cloud of red dust in his wake. "Maetrin," the man gasped, short of breath, "Enforcers—"

"Yes, I showed them in," the woman cut him off, trying to conceal the anxiety in her voice. I looked between them with interest. It seemed these *plivoi* were trying quite unsuccessfully to conceal something from us, although what they could possibly want to hide I couldn't begin to guess.

A moment later, another man followed the first through the door. Although he was also coated in rusty dirt, I realized after a second glance that this one was very young—an adolescent, maybe half a year older than me. It was difficult to tell, he was so filthy. This would be the apprentice. He seemed much more composed than his elders; he took me and then Ketros in with a quick movement of his gray eyes and stepped forward, placing three fingers over his brow.

"*Kyrii* Enforcers," he said smoothly, "to what do we owe the pleasure?"

"I won't take up too much of your time," Ketros replied, getting up from his seat. "We're here on behalf of the *geroi* in regards to your petitions for admittance to Bright Horizon. After a thorough review process conducted by the eugenics council, the *geroi* have decided that admittance will be granted to your apprentice, Eos."

The two older *plivoi* exhaled in relief, and the man smiled reassuringly at the boy until Ketros went on, "However, they have, unfortunately, opted to deny your own petitions—"

The woman blanched, her already shaky knees buckling beneath her. As her partner rushed to her side to support her, Eos stepped forward angrily. "What?!" he all but exploded. "There must be some kind of mistake!"

"No mistake," Ketros said, pulling up a System panel and rotating it to show the young man. The names and images of the two farmers appeared, both with the word "denied" printed below in the New Standard Script. I wasn't sure if the young man could read, but he seemed to get the gist, if his scornful glare was any indication.

"But, *Kyrios*," the older man protested faintly, "we've served the Iamoi faithfully our whole lives. This farm was once the most productive in the valley—"

"Correct," Ketros said. "Once. However, you must agree that you are now past your usefulness. Bright Horizon may be the second largest citidome on Iamos, but there is still only a limited amount of space. Food production is going to rely on new agricultural methods, not traditional farming." Ketros' voice was flat as he spoke, aloof and rehearsed. He'd given this speech a dozen times before, and he'd give it many more times before we were through. "The *geroi* greatly appreciate the contributions you have made to our people and our planet, but surely you must see that if we are to survive as a race, sacrifices must be made. Your time has come."

At this point the apprentice interrupted Ketros' monologue with a very loud and vehement curse. I gawked at him in shocked incredulity. Never in my life had I seen a *plivos* talk back to a *patros*. And this one didn't just argue, he was hurling obscenities. His nerve might be admirable if it wasn't so damned stupid.

"So what are you saying?" the apprentice raged. "You're just going to abandon them out here to die? Because of their *age*?! Maetrin and Phados get to smother to death out here with no air while even the oldest of the *patroi* live in comfort, safe in their precious domes?!"

"You need to watch your language, young man," Ketros snapped, his disinterest quickly replaced with hard fury. I noticed his hand had slipped down to the holster on his hip.

I stepped in hastily, trying to keep the situation in hand. "We will not be abandoning them to the elements," I explained, my voice level and firm. "In fact, in recognition of their years of service to our people, the *geroi* are offering them the option of a peaceful death by euthanasia"—I glanced over at the elders, who were looking resolutely at the floor—"which can be scheduled at your convenience."

Eos spluttered wordlessly at me for a moment, then asked, "That's supposed to make it better? Giving them the option to get put down like *animals*?"

"Look, I don't know what you're so upset about," I said. "The *geroi* granted *you* admittance to the dome."

"I don't care about that," Eos spat at me, and I doubled back in surprise. "Maetrin and Phados—"

"I have to say, boy, I'm a little concerned that you keep calling them that," Ketros said coldly. "You must have been born after the Progression. You know we don't use those words anymore. There are no parents on Iamos. None but the *geroi*."

The expression Eos gave Ketros was one that almost looked like pity. "I wouldn't expect a *patros* to understand," he growled. "*Patroi* don't understand things like love or loyalty."

This time, when Ketros reached for his holster, the farmers saw it. "No, please!" the woman begged as, simultaneously, the man shouted, "Wait!" and thrust himself between the Enforcer and Eos.

"Eos, stop this," the woman was saying to her apprentice, her voice full of emotions that I couldn't comprehend. "It doesn't matter what happens to us. He's right... we're past our usefulness. But there's a place for *you*, Eos."

"But what about," Eos began, and the woman sucked in her breath, a panic-stricken noise. I looked at her, my curiosity mingled with suspicion. Eos' eyes flicked to me for just a heartbeat; then he finished, as if it was what he'd meant all along, "you and Phados?"

A glimmer of movement out of the corner of my eye. I jerked my head around just in time to see the shadow disappear back into the hallway. But this time, I knew what I saw. My voice rose above the shouts of the *plivoi* and Ketros.

"Who was that boy?" I asked.

Everyone froze. The two farmers' already age-lightened skin paled considerably. For the first time, as Eos' eyes raked over me, I thought I saw a tinge of fear replacing the anger in them.

"What did you say?" Ketros asked.

Eos held my gaze for a long moment. His gray eyes seemed to be pleading with me, begging me not to repeat my question.

I looked away from him.

"I saw a boy in the next room," I answered, looking only at Ketros. "The records show that the only residents in this household are these two"—I gestured to the farmers—"and the apprentice, Eos. So. Who was that boy I saw?"

One more moment of silence; and then, suddenly, Eos yelled, "Run, Nikos!" He hurled himself away from us and into the next room.

"Stop!" I shouted, launching after him. Behind me, I heard

Ketros fumble with his holster as one of the farmers—I don't know which—slammed into him. There was a crash, and then the explosive sound of the weapon firing. I didn't waste my time to turn and see what happened. I simply tore after Eos, the muscles in my legs pumping as I ran.

Eos was already through the rear door of the residence, a cloud of red silt swirling through the air in his wake as he raced across the field of dust that stretched behind the house. Ahead of him, a little boy of about four or five years was running for his life, and the much taller Eos had nearly caught up to him. I darted across the field after them.

The boys were fast, but I was faster. I was almost upon them when Eos glanced over his shoulder at me. Without warning, the apprentice changed direction, slamming his body into mine.

The force of the impact knocked the air out of me, and I tumbled head over feet across the hard ground. Eos' weight pinned me down. I lashed out with my feet and felt a kick connect with the side of his face. He crumpled. I struggled out from under him and started to run after the boy once more, but Eos swung his own leg around, tripping me.

With me down again, Eos struggled to his own feet and, as I rose, he drew back his fist. I tried to swerve out of the way, but I wasn't fast enough, and his punch slammed into my jaw. The impact was so hard that the world flashed. It took a few seconds for my vision to correct itself. That was just enough time for Eos to wrench my arms around behind my back, twisted painfully, and hold me.

I furiously stomped down, grinding my heel into the top of his foot, but his thick boots prevented this from having much of an effect. I was enraged. This *plivoi* scum should never have been able to get the better of me, an apprentice Enforcer. But then again, most never would have tried. I supposed that fact alone had lulled me into complacency.

The younger boy was long gone by now. All that remained of him was the cloud of dust that was already disappearing in his wake, the wind quickly blowing away the tracks that he'd left and covering them with a layer of rusty silt.

"What do you think you stand to gain?" I spat. "You're not going to get away from us. Ketros is armed. He'll shoot you before he lets you escape."

"Yes, but you won't get *him*." Eos nodded in the direction the child had run. "I can promise you that."

"What is so special about that boy, that you're willing to sacrifice everything for him?"

"He's my brother," Eos answered without hesitation. "And that's something else you *patroi* wouldn't understand."

But I did understand, immediately. Those people in there, the ones that Eos was so insistent upon addressing as his parents... they had violated the eugenics statute. They had broken the most absolute law of the *geroi*. *They'd had a child.*

I was astounded. I didn't know how they could have done it; every person on Iamos—except for partners the eugenicists had selected for reproduction—was on mandatory birth control. It was in the very water we drank. I wondered dimly if the farmers had stumbled across some kind of water source that the *geroi* were unaware of, didn't control.

But *why*? The *gerotus* had adopted eugenics for a reason. The planet was *dying*. We simply didn't have the resources to sustain an uncontrolled population. It was a sacrifice that everyone had to make, for the good of our planet and our people. And the repercussions for violating the law were dire. I couldn't fathom why anyone would put themselves at such a risk for something so... *foolish.*

I said so aloud, and Eos laughed derisively. "They wanted it because it was their *right*, Enforcer."

"It was *not* their right," I argued. "The *geroi* —"

"The *geroi*," Eos scoffed. "The self-proclaimed saviors of Iamos. They don't care about the people, about saving the planet. All they care about is securing their own power. It doesn't matter to them how many good people die as long as they still have their cities of drudges they can control."

"What would your alternative be? Do you think any of us would be here right now if we'd had a choice about it? There is no *choice.* Iamos is dying. This is the only way."

"That's what the *geroi* want us to believe. It's what gives them their power. If everyone thinks that there is no alternative, they get to keep it."

I'd twisted around enough that I could see him over my shoulder. Eos wore an expression of condescension on his face that I knew mirrored my own when I'd first laid eyes on him, when he'd come in the door covered in dirt and grime. He said, "I saw you back there, looking at me like you're so much better than me, when the only real difference between us is the names the *geroi* call us by. The *geroi* took away your free will same as mine, but you act like they've given you some great gift just because you get to call yourself a *patroin* instead of a *plivoin.*"

I turned away from him, closed my eyes, but he kept right on talking, his insidious words clawing their way inside of me, poisoning me. "You can go ahead and play their little game, but not me. I *choose* not to let them control me," Eos hissed in my ear. "Every person is born with the right to *choose*. No person has the right to take away someone's freedom. They can try. But there will always be those who fight back. Phados, Maetrin— me—we chose to fight back. Because we'd rather die than give up our freedom."

While Eos was talking, I'd felt his grip on my wrists loosen. He didn't seem surprised when I wrenched away from him, twisted around, fists raised. He just looked at me, somberly. Waiting for my reply. Waiting to see if his words had affected me, or if he'd lost his fight.

"That's enough." I heard Ketros' voice from a distance. Both Eos and I turned and saw him standing in the doorway of the home, his weapon raised. "It's over, boy."

Eos said nothing. He simply walked back into the house. He didn't speak again; not when we found the *plivos'* lifeless body sprawled across the floor of the front room, the woman Eos called Maetrin weeping quietly over it. Not when we led the two survivors out to our *gurzas*, hands bound. Not one word, the whole long way back to Bright Horizon.

When we were back at the dome, Ketros and I were relieved of the charges, and Eos and the woman were taken into custody to await their sentences. I knew the pair of them would be dead before the end of the week. My stomach lurched abruptly at the thought that this fiery young man had had a chance at survival, and had thrown it all away.

I refused to look at him, but I felt Eos' eyes on me just before they led him away. He never spoke, but I still heard his voice ringing in my ears, echoing over and over.

Freedom.

I tried to put the encounter out of my mind, but it kept creeping back unbidden. Eos' words kept echoing through my head, treacherous as a *gamada*. Freedom. Choice. Those lofty concepts seemed so inconsequential when compared to the all-important need for *survival*. Regardless of the sacrifices it entailed, I couldn't fathom how anyone could find death preferable to life.

But one other thing was bothering me as well, and that is what ultimately brought me to the highest levels of the citidome that night. Here—without the ever-deepening buffer layers of rock or mudbrick that shielded most of the city, where the threat of solar radiation was at its greatest—was the place the *geroi* locked the dissenters. Those who violated the edicts, who could have no hope of appeal. Who would serve the collective greater with their deaths than with their lives.

I couldn't remember the last time I'd felt warm on Iamos, but the air in the upper levels was bitingly cold, far more than I was accustomed to. Even with my insulated clothing and the System regulating my body temperature, I felt goosebumps dance across my flesh. I sucked my breath in through my teeth. It was a wonder that the prisoners didn't freeze to death up here. Perhaps some of them did. It had never occurred to me to ask.

My presence in the prison was not remarked upon. The ranks of the Enforcers in Bright Horizon were not particularly numerous, and we each had a variety of assignments that took us everywhere in the citidome. The System recognized our genetic code, so no doors in the city were closed to us.

I found Eos huddled in the corner of a dingy cell, curled tightly in upon himself. He didn't move when I entered, and I half wondered if he was already dead. I nudged his still form roughly with my foot; eventually he stirred and looked up at me blearily. After a moment, his eyes came into focus and he realized who was standing over him. He tensed immediately.

"Enforcer. What do you want?"

"The truth," I replied. "Earlier, when you said things didn't have to be this way. What did you mean?"

"The truth is subjective. Do you want my truth, or the *geroi*'s?"

"Just answer my question."

His gray eyes held mine; my gaze didn't falter, and finally he dropped his own. He sighed. "All I meant was that there are other alternatives. Other ways to survive that don't involve all of us handing our lives over to the *geroi*."

"Such as?"

He rolled over on his side, looking away from me. It was a very child-like gesture, and it made me realize how young he really was—how young we both were. It seemed grossly unfair, suddenly, that he was going to die before he'd ever really lived.

But have you lived, either?

"It's just a legend, really," Eos said. "A rumor. But... there's talk among the *plivoi*. That maybe the *geroi*'s scientists were wrong. That maybe there really is a way to stop the atmosphere from depleting. That maybe Iamos can be saved after all."

I was confused. "But if there were a way to stop this, wouldn't the *geroi* have tried it?"

"If the planet were saved, there'd be no need for the *geroi* anymore," Eos pointed out.

My legs felt weak, and unconsciously I sank to my knees on the floor beside him. "Surely they couldn't," I protested. "I mean, they say it themselves. They remind us every day. '*All lives are one.*' We live for one another."

"Do we, Enforcer?" Eos asked. His tone made it clear that this wasn't really a question. "Or do we live for the *geroi*?"

I must have known the answer already, deep down. If I hadn't had my doubts, I never would have come here tonight. Eos' words in the desert would not have affected me. Perhaps I knew all along, in my heart of hearts, that the *geroi*'s promises were too good to be true. Still, I couldn't stop the question that spilled from my lips next.

"How do you know?"

Eos sighed, rolled over, sat upright with his back against the mudbrick wall. His eyes stared unseeingly at the ceiling. "I don't know. All I know is that I want to try. Because this life the *geroi* are giving us now... it's not a life. How can it be, when we have no power over our own fates?" He closed his eyes. "There's only one thing in this world that we have, Enforcer, and it's our own lives. I won't let another person control mine for me. If I can't choose how to live or who to love, I'd rather not live at all."

I could hear air moving through the halls outside, and another chill ran across my skin. I shivered, pulling my knees up into my chest and holding them tightly. Then I said, "Your... brother. Your parents. You love them?"

He didn't look at me. "Yes."

Love. That was another word that didn't have a place on

Iamos anymore—along with *freedom* and *choice*. Things worth living for. Things worth dying for.

"Where do you think your brother is now?" I asked idly. I didn't expect him to answer, since the response could lead the Enforcers to Nikos' hiding spot.

But then he spoke, softly, barely audible. "There's a place… just a legend, probably. It's called Elytherios."

I repeated the word, uncertain I'd heard him correctly. "That's in the old language, isn't it?"

Eos nodded, a crooked smile playing at his lips. "It means 'freedom.'" When I simply looked down, he continued, "It's a safe haven for refugees, a place the *geroi* can't find. Supposedly the renegade scientists went there first, the ones whose research violated the edicts. A hidden place, beyond the rock spire plains. And"—he moved his eyes to me without moving his head, a sideways glance—"I know it sounds crazy, but they say the scientists found a way to make the plants grow again. And if the plants grow, then the atmosphere… they might be able to heal Iamos."

I shook my head. "It can't be real. If there was a way to fix Iamos, surely the *geroi* would…" I trailed off at his scoff, switched tactics. "Either way, if such a place existed, surely we would know about it! The System has the planet cataloged, there's nowhere they could hide an entire city."

"You'd be amazed how easy it is to trick a mind that's become so reliant on the System."

I stared at Eos, bewildered. "What's that supposed to mean?"

He smirked. "It's just something I heard one time."

I sighed in exasperation. "So, that's where you think Nikos is now? Elytherios?"

Eos' lopsided grin faded. "I don't know where he is now. The plan was for me to take him there myself, and that Maetrin and Phados would meet up with us later. We knew that there was no hope for Maetrin and Phados to get into Bright Horizon. Even if they had, there was no way they could have kept Nikos hidden. But we didn't think the Enforcers would come this early. We thought for sure the *geroi* would wait until after the harvest."

I stared down at my toes, feeling guilty in spite of myself. It was ridiculous that I should care about the plight of this *plivos* and his family of lawbreakers, but...

I did care. I couldn't help it. I cared.

All lives are one.

"Do you really think that Elytherios exists?" I asked at last.

Eos didn't answer for a long moment. When he finally spoke, he didn't meet my eyes. "Yes."

I sighed, gnawing uncomfortably on my lip. Here it was, then. Something I'd never wanted, and never asked for. But realizing that it was *mine* filled me with an unexpected spark of life; it was as if I'd been sleeping all these years, and I had been suddenly, rudely awakened.

I had a choice.

Getting them out of their cells and then out of the citidome was no small matter. I was lucky, I supposed, to have been trained with the Enforcers. Seeing without being seen was one of our specialties. Silently moving in the shadows, manipulating the System to plant false evidence—I was skilled at it all. Maetrin and Eos were scheduled for execution in the morning. A small tweak to the System meant simply that the records showed the execution had already been carried out. Between the upsurge in euthanizations and the routine execution of dissidents, two nondescript *plivoi* would never be noticed. For all intents and purposes, they would be dead.

If I had faith in one thing, it was my own abilities. No one would connect me with this disappearance, if they noticed it at all.

The stolen *gurzas'* hot breath came out in puffs of steam as we stood in the ice-cold shadows outside Bright Horizon. I looked up at Eos, and he down at me. "Will you be able to navigate without your earpiece?" I asked finally, feeling a bit pathetic. I wasn't skilled at farewells; until now, there was no one I cared about enough to say goodbye to.

"We'll be fine," Eos assured me. "The *patroi* would probably be scandalized to hear it, but we *plivoi* are far less reliant on the System than the rest of you. We're better at surviving than you give us credit for."

I laughed feebly, glancing over my shoulder for any sign that the other Enforcers were on to me. Maetrin had moved her *gurza* to the edge of the dome's shadow and was watching me, her gaze heavy with distrust. I knew she didn't believe my offer of help was genuine. I couldn't blame her; I had been, after all, responsible for the death of her partner, if nothing else. If I hadn't alerted Ketros to Nikos' presence, none of this ever would have happened.

I'd had a choice then, too. My whole life, I realized with a twinge, had been full of little choices, and I'd never noticed it. I'd chosen to follow the *geroi*. I'd chosen to enforce the edicts. Choice after choice after choice.

Is that what freedom means?

"You'd better hurry," I said, "before the Enforcers catch you."

Eos nodded and guided his *gurza* toward Maetrin's. I watched him, and thought, *I hope you find Elytherios.*

Then Eos paused, turning back to face me. "Enforcer," he began hesitantly.

"It's Marin," I corrected. We'd come too far for him to address me by my rank any longer. Besides, the title no longer seemed to fit me.

That crooked smile again. "Marin, then." He looked anxiously at Maetrin, then back at me. "You don't have to stay here, you know."

I stared at him for a moment, uncomprehending. He nudged the *gurza* forward, close enough that his words could be heard by no one but the two of us. "You've come this far," Eos said. "It could be all that's waiting for us out there is a cold death in the mountains, but... you have a choice."

Another choice.

In Bright Horizon, I led a life to be envied. I was soon to be *enilin*, and my apprenticeship was almost complete. Under the *geroi*, I would be guaranteed a life of comfort and security. Wealth, prestige, anything a person could hope for would be at my fingertips. My birthright.

What awaited me out there? We'd be chasing a fairy tale. More likely than not, Elytherios didn't even exist. The odds were a million to one that there was nothing waiting for us in those mountains but death.

And freedom.

I closed my eyes and saw my future unfolding before me in

two different directions: one a long, straight road, even and safe; the other a short, craggy trail leading to nowhere. To even consider it was complete lunacy.

But it was a choice.

I pulled out my earpiece. It was the one thing that bound me to the System—to the *geroi*, to the citidome, to Iamos. For an odd, disjointed moment, it seemed I was holding my very life in my hand, and I looked down at it in wonder.

Then I dropped the earpiece to the ground and crushed it beneath my heel.

"I choose freedom."

ACKNOWLEDGMENTS

There aren't enough words to thank everyone who's been a part of making this book a reality, but I'm going to try anyway.

Thank you to all the readers who enjoyed *Fourth World* and made this story a possibility. Your support and patience mean so much to me. Hopefully the wait for the next book will be much shorter! I hope you will join me for the ride.

Thank you to my family, especially to my mom, for all your encouragement. Huge thanks also to my sister for being the world's biggest shipper and ordering me back in 2013 to make this story a priority. It's always great to have someone to share your rabid fangirl tendencies with, and when it's for your own original series? It's the best thing in the universe.

Thank you to *Ama-gi* Magazine, Students for Liberty, and the Libertarian Fiction Authors for publishing the original version of "The Choice" and naming it one of the Ten Best Short Stories of 2014. That opportunity started my publishing career and was a wonderful beginning to the Iamos journey.

Thank you to the Hit-and-Run gang as well as everyone in #Writing for your inspiration for the Martian Anarchy Brigade. I kind of stole a little bit of all of you for Henry (the nice parts—his jerkish side is all me). Hope you don't mind.

An extra-special thank you to my editor, Rose Anne Roper, for polishing my words until they shine; and to Najla Qamber for the most beautiful cover I could have ever dreamed of.

Thanks also to George Donnelly, Claudie Arseneault, Lauren Jankowski, Darcie Little Badger, Joel Cornah, Karen Teal, and especially my almost-sister Selenia Paz, for all the subtle and not-so-subtle ways you've helped me on my writing journey. You guys are the best.

And finally, thank you to the Leopards for starting it all.

ABOUT THE AUTHOR

Lyssa Chiavari is an author of speculative fiction for young adults, including the critically-acclaimed *Fourth World*, the first book in the Iamos Trilogy. Her short fiction has appeared in *Ama-gi* magazine, *Wings of Renewal*, *Clarion Call*, and *Perchance to Dream*, an anthology of YA Shakespeare retellings which she also edited. When she's not writing—which isn't often—you can usually find her exploring the woods near her home in the Pacific Northwest or losing an unreasonable number of life balloons on Donkey Kong. Visit Lyssa on the web at lyssachiavari.com.

.

ALSO BY LYSSA CHIAVARI

the iamos trilogy

Book One: *Fourth World*
Book Two: *New World*
Book Three: *One World*

other novels

Cheerleaders from Planet X

short fiction

"Gale"
*Perchance to Dream: Classic Tales From
the Bard's World in New Skins*

"Seven Years Among Dragons"
Wings of Renewal: A Solarpunk Dragon Anthology

"CinderellA.I."
Magic at Midnight: A YA Fairy Tale Anthology

"Sea-Stars and Sand Dollars"
Brave New Girls: Tales of Heroines Who Hack

Find more of Lyssa's short fiction at
Patreon.com/LyssaChiavari

PRAISE FOR FOURTH WORLD
book one of the iamos trilogy

"*Fourth World* is a gem. Exciting and interesting while covering the span of archaeology, time travel, government conspiracies, overcoming diversity, individualism, and friendships that defy odds, Chiavari paints us a vivid colonized Mars with such beauty it's effortless to believe."

- Brenda J. Pierson, author of JOYTHIEF

"Striking characters evolving in a beautifully-described Mars, coherent and entrancing world-building, a mystery that builds relentlessly, one question after the other..."

- Claudie Arseneault, author of CITY OF STRIFE

"This book fires perfectly on all cylinders."

- Jaylee James, editor of VITALITY magazine

"The world-building of both the Martian colony and Nadin's world, Iamos, is nothing short of spectacular. Full of mysteries, intrigue, and fantastical new discoveries, *Fourth World* is the kind of book that's hard to put down."

- Mary Fan, author of STARSWEPT

Printed in Great Britain
by Amazon